I0763549

# II: MARSHMALLOW

# II: MARSHMALLOW

*Short Stories from The Lie of Innocence, of which Book One is The Homestead*

QUINTUS H. GOULD

Ancile Press

First published in Great Britain in 2023 by Ancile Press.



A CIP catalogue record for this title is available from the British Library.

ISBN 9781739217242
eBook ISBN 9781739217259

Ancile Press
71 - 75 Shelton Street
Covent Garden
London
WC2H 9JQ

ancilepress.co.uk

# Contents

# French Onion Soup

*Some three years before The Homestead, Alexander celebrates his eighteenth birthday.*

It had been the summer she had broken her arm. Fifteen years old, terrorised by adolescent frustrations and insecurities, she had been forced to stay indoors after the front wheel of her bicycle caught on an exposed tree root. She had gone over the handlebars and, hands outstretched to catch herself, had heard the bone break before she felt the pain. Crying all the way up to the house, Robert had soon realigned it. *A closed oblique fracture to the radius bone.* Afterwards, she was banned from the bicycle, both by her father and the plaster cast on her arm. Immobilised, she had spent seven weeks in the house, sitting on the sofa for hours at a time, reading and drinking infinite cups of tea as she was told nonsense stories by the old man.

When he first brought her a book, she had been surprised. Once upon a time, she wouldn't have been, *but things had changed since then.* A nod and she had taken it from him, grateful in more ways than one, her own reserve having been all but exhausted. He had left her after that, but she had noticed him, the evening of that same day, watching her struggle to turn the pages as she gripped the book with one hand. Two days later, he came to her again with another book. That time, he had offered to read it with her, and so they had sat, side-by-side on the sitting room sofa, in silence, as he turned the pages for the two of them. Outside, the Sun had been higher in the sky than it had been all year, both of their bicycles abandoned in the garage.

'Happy birthday.'

She handed him the present. It was wrapped in tissue paper and she kept her eyes on it as he took it from her. He thanked her, then tore the paper, exposing the journal which she had wrapped for him only the night before.

'It's from a gift shop in town,' she said as he looked at its cover. A rich reproduction of a Victorian lithograph, it was populated by sketches of starfish, the sorts of scientific illustrations synonymous with oceanographers. The grey-green sea star at the centre was covered in spikes and boasted purple tips on its arms.

Alexander turned the journal over in his hands. 'Thanks,' he said again, this time raising his eyes to look at her.

Mary nodded. For a second she thought she saw him, but, a blink, and he forgot everything. Behind her, there were others waiting to give their gifts. He placed the journal on the table with the other presents he'd unwrapped, and she walked away.

The day before, Mary had stood outside, her arms folded across her chest, as everyone waited for Alexander to emerge from D Building. Almost as soon as they had all walked down from the house to the habitation buildings, it had started to rain. A torrent of heavy, beating water, a cloud had burst right over them. Only ten minutes before, the weather had been perfect. And so, her cardigan left up at the house, she had been shivering by the time Alexander eventually came through the door of the grey-clad building. A young boy followed him and, there, on the wet grass, in front of everyone who had travelled to witness it, Alexander slaughtered him. The eve of his eighteenth birthday, it had been expected of him.

Now, the bad weather of the day before replaced by sunshine, it was almost time to eat.

'Go and talk with some of the others, marshmallow. I can manage.' Looking up from the large pot that she was stirring, Sophie smiled at her across the kitchen. There were bowls arranged on the table in the centre of the room; Mary straightened the last in a row so as to put it in line with the rest.

'I'm alright,' she said, glancing Alexander's mother. 'I'm here to help.'

Sophie reached for the ladle on the worktop beside the stove. Immersing it in the liquid, she assessed the thickness of the soup before turning again to the young woman standing by the table.

'You should go and speak with Sabine,' Sophie continued. Dressed in navy blue polka dot, her hair was tucked behind her ears. 'Ever since—' a pause and she sighed. She returned the ladle to the worktop and, slowly, turned so that she was resting against it. Hands crossed over her apron, she was holding herself. 'Poor Papa—' she whispered. Another sigh and, looking at Mary, Sophie smiled weakly.

Slowly, Mary nodded.

'I know,' Sophie said, her tone brightening, 'why don't you two sit together at the table? It must have been a while since you girls had a proper chat. It will give you a chance to catch up whilst Robert, Grandpa and your father talk about the usual nonsense.'

At that, Mary smiled. 'Alright,' she said.

'Good,' Sophie beamed. 'Now, go on! I'll come and find you if I need you.'

A nod and Mary turned to leave.

'Oh, and marshmallow—'

Mary looked over her shoulder.

'If you can manage to draw Robert away from the others,' Sophie said, smiling at her from the stove, 'tell him I'll need his help in the next five minutes.'

Still smiling, Mary said she would and, with that, left the kitchen.

The front of the house was busy, as was the hallway to the back, and even the steps away from the door and into the garden. There were people everywhere, family members, and extended family members, and friends of the family, and people she had never seen or heard of before. Close to a rose-heavy arch which shaded an old bench, her father was standing with Alexander's, laughing together as they listened to another man share an amusing anecdote. Mary pulled her cardigan tighter around her torso and slipped through the crowd to reach them. When her father saw her, he called her name and held out his hand for her to take.

'How are you, my love?' Ern asked as he drew her to him.

Mary said she was fine and offered a meagre smile to him,

and then the others in the group. There was nodding and reciprocal smiling.

'Robert—' Mary turned to Alexander's father, 'Sophie asked for you to go in and help.'

'Of course,' Robert said with a nod. Hands in front of him, he was wearing a buckled, black cotton contraption over his shirt. Tightened over his shoulders and around his front, it contained his youngest child, the fair-haired, fair-faced toddler, Aurélie. An affectionate pat of her back and Robert, with a word, excused himself from the group, leaving Mary to listen to more anecdotes with her father. Something about the quality of timber. Then, someone told a joke and triggered an eruption of guffawing. Unmoved, Mary quietly rested her head against her father's arm.

Alexander was standing on the other side of the lawn. Entertaining a group of his own, he was surrounded by his sister, his cousins, and all the other young people who had travelled along with their parents for his birthday celebrations. It was his coming of age, and everyone wanted to be a part of it.

Mary breathed deeply.

Like his father only a moment ago, he laughed when someone said something funny. The rest of the group giggled along too, the dark-haired teenage girl standing at Alexander's side clapping as they did. There was tummy gripping, and Alexander's little sister, Guinevere, began to dance in the excitement, inciting her cousin to continue clapping. Another girl in the group joined in, resulting in some of the boys pulling faces, provoking the laughter all over again. Still leaning against Ern, Mary noticed that Alexander was the first of the group to stop laughing.

'Food's almost ready to be served!'

Mary raised her head from her father's arm.

'If you could start taking your seats, please!' Robert was standing by the back door. His two-year-old daughter still strapped to his chest, he extended his arms as he addressed his guests. 'The first course will be out shortly.' Brown eyes bright, he smiled at everyone before returning inside.

As she watched Robert go back into the house, Mary felt her father move away from her. A man, the same one who had told the amusing anecdote, patted him on the arm and, drawing him into a discussion, led him towards one of the tables which had been arranged on the back lawn of the Wheatleighs' house. Head bobbing up and down in lively conversation, Ern pulled a handkerchief from his trouser pocket as he sat at the table. A quick moment to blow his nose, and he continued talking to the other man, his daughter watching them from a distance as they grinned, then chuckled, then arranged themselves in their chairs.

Eyes crossing the lawn, Mary saw Alexander and the dark-haired girl, his cousin Sabine, move towards another of the tables. They were talking together and walked slowly, neither one of their faces as animated as they had been a few minutes ago. When they reached a section of empty chairs, they stopped. As everyone else moved to take their seats, Mary watched Alexander's hand run down the side of his face. He said something, and his cousin, shaking her head, reached for his hand. He nodded then, and, shrugging his shoulders, offered Sabine a smile. All around them, the rest of the party was laughing and loud.

Mary would wait for him to take his seat next to his

grandfather before going over to Sabine. *He doesn't want to see me* — after so many years, she knew that. Only, he didn't go. He stayed talking with his cousin, even as everyone else — most seated, some still dawdling to chairs — clapped in response to the appearance of the first course. And so, tucking her hair behind her ears, Mary hurried out of the path of the soup bowls to the table.

Sabine smiled when she saw her. Alexander merely tilted his chin in her direction, his face expressionless.

'Sit next to me?' Sabine asked Mary, already placing a hand on her arm so as to guide her towards the two empty chairs behind which she and Alexander stood. She was clearly happy to have Mary there, and, still holding onto her, energetically offered one of the chairs to her. Alexander quickly stepped out of his cousin's way, his arm brushing Mary's as he did.

'Sorry,' he said to her.

Mary just nodded. As it was, they almost never spoke.

'We were talking about Guinevere,' Sabine explained as she, hands on Mary's shoulders, settled her on the chair. 'About how strange she's been acting ever since—' she stopped and, a grin pushing out the corners of her mouth, laughed. Her teeth showing, Sabine lowered her face to Mary's. 'About how strange she's been ever since Elliott arrived,' she whispered. A breathy giggle and she moved her eyes from Mary's to elsewhere at the table. Dressed in a pretty-patterned, pink dress, Alexander's nine-year-old sister was delicately arranging a napkin on her lap, snatching glances at a boy sitting further down the table as she did.

Following Sabine's gaze, a slow smile quirked Mary's lips.

'She's been showing off even more than usual,' Sabine

continued as she sat down beside Mary. 'Dancing.' A laugh. 'Singing.' She stretched the sound of the word, then turned her head to her cousin. 'Hasn't she, Alex?'

Still standing next to Mary's chair, he didn't say anything. Elsewhere at the table, soup was being served. Both his grandmother and grandfather already had bowls in front of them.

'I'd best sit down,' Alexander said to Sabine.

She nodded. 'Okay, Alex.'

A small smile and he moved away. Passing the chairs of others as he walked, he was forced to stop and entertain compliments and congratulations. There was hand-shaking, and one old lady made him bend down to receive a kiss. She pulled him by the cheeks and, at the last moment, twisted his face so as to peck him straight on the lips. Lipstick the same colour as his cheeks, he stumbled away as everyone else laughed. Silent in her seat, Mary watched as he went. From where she had been standing before, it hadn't looked as though he and Sabine had been talking about Guinevere.

'What soup is it?'

Mary turned to Alexander's cousin. She was smiling at her.

'What flavour is it?' she asked.

'French onion,' Mary replied.

'That's my favourite,' Sabine said, nodding.

Mary opened her napkin and draped it over her knees. 'Yes,' she murmured. 'It's Alexander's, too.'

Just ahead of them, Sophie was presenting bowls to her guests, lifting them from the tray in her hands so as to place them on the white tablecloth. At her side was Sabine's mother with another tray of soup.

'What do you think you'll have for yours?'

Sabine was smiling at her again.

Slowly, Mary shuffled in her chair. 'I haven't thought about it,' she said.

'It's only a few months away.' Sabine shook her head, unconvinced. 'Surely you must have?'

The soups were moving closer.

'Not really.'

Sabine laughed. 'I don't believe that.'

Sophie was only a couple of places away from them now. As she placed yet another bowl of soup on the table, Sabine leant forward in her seat. '*Tata*—'

Looking up from the food, Sophie smiled at her. 'What is it, dear?'

'Mary says she hasn't decided about her birthday yet. About what food to have.'

Alexander's mother stepped towards them. She rearranged the tray so that it was balanced on the edge of the table. Either side of her, guests shuffled their cutlery to make room for it.

'Oh dear,' Sophie sighed and, upon looking at Mary, smiled. 'Yes.' Another smile, this one softer. 'But, you shall have to decide soon, marshmallow, or I won't be able to arrange it all in time.'

Mary just nodded. On the other side of the table, a blue-tied man was already slurping his soup. A quick dab of his mouth with his napkin and he cleared his throat. 'Well, this soup is perfect, Sophie.' He looked up at his hostess and nodded. 'I wholeheartedly recommend a repeat if Miss. Stansfield is having trouble choosing.'

Readjusting the tray, Sophie turned to smile at the man. 'Thank you, Eugene.'

To her right, another, also sipping from a spoon, added their own approval.

Again, Sophie smiled and expressed her thanks. 'I'm certain Mary will consider your endorsement, too, Jasper.' She reached for a bowl on the tray and, leaning across the table, placed it in front of Mary. 'It's an important decision for such a memorable occasion.' Another bowl, and she presented soup to Sabine. Her tray now empty, Sophie tucked it under her arm and took a moment to look at Mary. Meeting her eyes, she smiled and said, 'It doesn't have to be French onion, marshmallow.' Soft, generous eyes. 'It doesn't even have to be soup.'

Swallowing a breath, Mary simply said, 'It's alright. I like soup.'

The man with the blue tie was happy about that, as was the second man, and several other guests within proximity of the conversation. As they delighted in discussion of a repeat of Alexander's eighteenth birthday, Mary lifted her spoon from the tablecloth and scooped a toasted, cheese-crusted crouton from the surface of the liquid. Next to her, Sabine was enjoying a chunk of broth-sweetened onion.

*Ever in his shadow.*

Mary swallowed the crouton.

It hadn't always been that way.

Many years earlier, she and Alexander had been inseparable. Torchlight secrets and tickle fights. Sneaking into places they both knew they shouldn't have, then blackmailing each other about it afterwards. Snowmen in the winter and woodland dens in the summer. Stealing food from the fridge.

Eating it when everyone else was asleep. Rock pools and spiny starfish.

*Promises of eternity.*

Back then, they had both been young enough not to worry about what might come later. A little boy and a little girl who never even stopped to question the meaning of friendship, let alone anything else. And so, the same Sun in the same sky, neither one had eclipsed the other. Then, one day, everything changed. The innocence of youth was spent, and she was left to trawl the rock pools alone. A hallucinatory spectre, she was banished to the shadows.

*Until that summer.*

It had lasted all of seven weeks. The same length of time that the plaster cast had been on her arm. A book open on a pillow between them, both of their backs had been straight against the sofa, neither one daring to turn their heads lest they catch sight of each other. He had confirmed that she was finished reading before turning the pages, until they had fallen into rhythm with each other and he didn't need to ask anymore. Whenever he flipped the page, his hand had brushed against hers, until, eventually, it had just settled there, knuckle-to-knuckle on the sitting room sofa, in an awkward, and yet somehow still comfortable, silence. One time, she had fallen asleep. Pain medication and back-to-back hours pretending to read. He had woken her by touching her face, and, looking him in the eye, she had seen — *just for an instant* — that the promises had never been broken.

When the plaster cast was removed and he had stopped spending time with her, she had asked him why. He had told her that it hadn't meant anything, and that he had just felt sorry for her. That night, sobbing against her pillow, screaming into it, begging for her arm to break all over again, she had told herself he couldn't possibly hurt her any more than he already had.

Two years later, slipping out of her cardigan as the warmth of the French onion soup settled in her stomach, no one would have been able to guess that Mary had once broken her arm. There was no scar. Time, so it seemed, was able to heal most things.

Pushing out her chair, Mary placed her napkin on the table and stood up.

'Did you want me to come with you?' Sabine asked from the chair next to hers.

Mary shook her head. 'I'm alright, thank you. I won't be long.' Draping her cardigan over her arm, she walked across the grass to the back door of the house. Around her, others were either finishing or had already finished their soup and were likewise looking to stretch their legs before the next course.

There were loiterers outside the downstairs bathroom. Everyone wanted to talk to everyone, and so she had to duck and dodge conversations all the way along the hallway to the stairs. Rushing up to her bedroom, she slipped through the door, threw her cardigan onto the bed, and went into her bathroom.

*There is no way it can hurt any more.*

Two impassive grey eyes stared back at her from the mirror. A curl out of place. She pushed it back. Breathing. After that, she washed her hands and left the room. Leaving her cardigan on the bed, she quickly straightened the waist of her skirt before hurrying back out through her bedroom door.

They very almost walked into each other.

'Sorry—'

'I'm sorry—'

'I didn't—'

'You go first.' He gestured away from them to the stairs.

'Are you sure?'

He nodded.

'Thanks.'

She walked down the stairs without looking back up at him. As she passed the kitchen, she caught sight of Sophie moving to the stove, fretting to Robert, fussing about the food.

'Do you need any help?' Mary asked, poking her head through the door.

'No, dear,' Sophie looked across the room at her. 'Thank you.'

Mary nodded. Behind her, there was shuffling on the rug.

'Do you need me now?'

Again, Sophie turned her face to the open door. Quiet, and Mary withdrew into the shadow of the hallway so as to allow Alexander into the kitchen.

'Is it time yet?' he asked his mother. His voice was low and he started fiddling with the edge of the oak sideboard that stood beside the door. 'Or should I go back outside?'

'No, my strawberry,' Sophie smiled at him. 'You'd best stay in here now.'

Alexander nodded.

Oven-gloved and ready, his father was waiting by the

cooker. The room filled with steam when he opened the door to the main oven. Carefully, he guided the tray out of the heat and onto the waiting trivet. From the doorway, Mary could smell the meat.

There was a large blue and white porcelain platter standing on the table, and it was onto that that Sophie arranged the cuts. As she did, the kitchen moved about her: Sabine's mother arrived to carry away a tray laden with potatoes; Robert spooned carrot rounds and broccoli florets into bowls from the steamer pans on the stove; Sophie's brother made an appearance so as to shuffle more napkins outside; and Alexander was directed towards little dishes of cranberry sauce and mustard. The rest of the food had already been delivered to the tables at the back of the house. By the door, Mary simply watched, waiting to be useful.

When Sophie was finished, she invited Alexander to come to the porcelain platter on the table. He finished preparing the last dish of cranberry sauce, placing it onto the waiting tray, then moved to her side.

'You'll need these, dear,' his mother said, pushing a pair of kitchen tongs into his hand. 'Just put them on the plate when you— Well—' a sigh and she smiled at him. 'You know what to do, my strawberry.' With that, Sophie stood back and, after taking a moment to look at him, tweaked her son's nose.

'Thank you, my darling.' Stepping away from the vegetables, Robert placed his hand on the small of his wife's back. 'You've done an excellent job, as ever.'

Sophie turned to him and smiled. An intake of breath and she again looked at Alexander. 'Well, then,' she said, 'I'll walk the broccoli to the table.' A quick nod at the doorway and Mary was instructed to take the tray containing the condiments. She did and, as they left the kitchen together, Sophie pulled the door shut. Turning, Mary saw Robert reach to place his hand on Alexander's shoulder just as the wood kissed the frame.

'Come on, dear,' Sophie smiled at her. Blue polka dot, and her eyes crinkled at the corners. They walked out to the back garden together.

Once the broccoli and carrots and cranberry and mustard were suitably spread amongst the tables, it didn't take long for Alexander to reappear with his father. Walking in front as Robert held the back door open for him, he was holding the blue and white platter in both his hands, eyes straight ahead and set on their destination.

Somehow taller than he had been the afternoon before, his hair was combed and his shirt creaseless as he carried the meat across the grass. Everyone stopped to watch him. Any conversations that had been flowing paused, and glasses were returned to the tablecloth. A nose that had been in the middle of being blown was abandoned, and children were encouraged to hush. Someone sucked in a breath, and someone else swallowed a sneeze. The full length of every table, eyes — some young, some old, some in between — were still and did not blink. At the head of one, one pair, grey and serious and older than most, waited for the platter to be set down on the tablecloth in front of them. When it was, they looked from the meat on the porcelain to the face of the young man who had presented it to them.

'Grandpa,' Alexander addressed the owner of the eyes.

The old man sat forward in his chair and cleared his throat. 'Alexander.'

Keeping his head raised, Alexander slowly lowered himself to the ground so that he was kneeling on the grass in front of his grandfather. 'I have brought you this food,' he began, his voice quiet but confident, 'to say thank you for all of the food you have brought me. And—' a wobble and Alexander took a quick breath of air. 'And to show you that I am prepared and able to do the same.'

Their eyes still on each other's, Robert Senior nodded. Then, louder than his grandson, he said, 'I receive this food from you to acknowledge that you are prepared and able to provide, as I have provided for you.'

Silent, Alexander kept his eyes on his grandfather's.

'And,' the old man continued, 'in front of everyone who has come here to witness, to recognise you, Alexander Robert Wheatleigh, as a man.'

Almost as soon as he had pronounced the final word, Robert Senior raised up his right hand from the arm of his chair and, drawing it up across his chest, swung it down in a single, solid movement to strike the side of his grandson's face. There was a crack as the back of his hand met the young man's cheek, but no other sound. Alexander, eyes still forward, received the blow in silence.

'So you do not forget what that means,' the old man said to him, in the same serious voice as before, 'and so others know that you will not flinch or turn from what must be done.'

A second of silence, like a sudden intake of breath, and then the party burst into applause. Shouting, of best wishes and good luck, rang out from the tables, with some men pushing back their chairs and standing so as to bring their hands together in broader, louder ovation. Sustained in their appreciation, Alexander's guests cheered all the more when he stood, raised from the grass by his father who, having waited behind his son until that moment, stepped forward to place a hand on his shoulder and coax him from the ground. In front of him, his grandfather, still seated in his chair, clapped too, slower than the others, but without moving his eyes from Alexander's. At the old man's side, his wife clutched a handkerchief, dabbing tears from her eyes as their daughter-in-law moved from her own chair to embrace her son.

'I'm so very proud of you, my strawberry,' Sophie whispered into Alexander's chest as she held him. Nodding, he wrapped his arms around his mother and waited for the celebrations to subside. Eventually, he released her and, greeted by his father's smiling, brown eyes, picked up the kitchen tongs from the platter of meat he had placed on the table.

Alexander looked down at his grandfather in his chair. 'What would you like, Grandpa?' he asked him, gesturing to the platter with the tongs.

'How about the genitals, lad?' A wicked smile and Robert Senior, seriousness dissipated, immediately barked a laugh. 'Oh, come on,' he chortled at his grandson, 'don't look so shell-shocked. Just give me a good old hunk of meat—' he wafted his hand towards the thick, fat-edged slices in the middle of the platter. 'There you go,' he said, nodding, 'and another one.'

Alexander shuffled a second slice of meat onto his grandfather's plate. As he did, he was watched by the grey-haired lady seated at the table next to him. Dressed in a delicate lilac blouse, her eyes were big and brown, and gleamed when he turned to look at her.

'Grandma?' Alexander asked, tongs still in hand.

'Less than Grandpa for me, sweetpea,' she said.

Alexander nodded and pinched a piece of flesh between the tongs. She smiled and thanked him. When he was done, Robert stepped in to lift the platter from the table. Securing the heavy weight in both hands, he smiled at his mother before encouraging his son forward and on towards the next guest. Just as with his grandparents, Alexander asked them which of the meat they wanted. Loin, rib, leg and shank, there was enough for everyone to sample his harvest.

As Alexander moved down the main table, Mary rearranged her napkin and shuffled her chair closer to Sabine's. She was telling her about a trip she and her mother had just taken together. Haberdasheries and cream teas overlooking the river, her brother and father had stayed at home. She was learning how to bullion stitch, and had recently scallop-edged a new cardigan. Mary nudged her chair closer again. On the other side of her, wine was being drained from glasses and conversations were getting louder. Olive Merino wool, and Sabine paused for a drink. Mary glanced down the table. No closer than he had been before, Alexander was waiting for his father to finish talking before serving the next person.

*How long am I willing to wait?*

In any other respect, it would have been a rational question. *But not in this.* An exhilarating, exasperating, exhausting excess of emotion, she wished she didn't love him, was sometimes so furious that she wanted to hate him, but it was not something over which she had any control. Unhinged, unrequited feeling that drove her to the edge of insanity, the slightest action was enough to pull her back, *until every almost smile becomes a redeemer.* An archeologist scrambling in the mud, constantly on the lookout, frantically searching for the secret symbol that only she could interpret, a sign that the ancient language was not yet extinct, she was miserable most of the time. Yet, there was no changing it: she couldn't remember the first day that she had felt it, and therefore couldn't imagine the last. And so, for as long as the voice inside her head and the pain in her heart told her that it was true, there was nothing that she could do other than love him.

'What would you like?'

She blinked and he was in front of her.

'A chop, please.'

He nodded and placed it on her plate.

*An almost smile.*

He moved to the person next to her.

*But he has forgotten everything.*

But she hadn't. Unread books and spiny starfish, strawberry marshmallows and ridiculous childhood drawings, bicycles, board games, blackberry bushes, hunting for treasure and swimming in the sea together, chasing each other in the rain and days of melted ice cream. *Promises of eternity.* It was exhausting to have to feel so much, but she hadn't forgotten.

*And so, there is no way it can hurt any more.*

Picking up her knife and fork from the tablecloth, Mary cut into the meat. Next to her, Sabine was once again talking about her birthday and what sort of a menu she would like.

'French onion soup.'

Mary cut off another piece of meat.

Whatever she decided, whatever else she could have wanted, it would be French onion soup.

# White Knight

*It is the Wheatleighs' annual New Year's party, and the precursor to Alexander's lamented nine-month absence from home — the parallel to Strawberry's Seasick.*

'Value and purchasing power are fundamentally connected. You cannot remove the latter and expect the former to withstand.'

A stretched, scoffing smile and the young man straightened his back. 'Nonsense,' he said. 'Even purchasing power emerges from assigned, consensual value. Do away with the commodity and the value remains.'

The grinning young woman in front of him shook her head. 'For a time, perhaps. But, ultimately, the success of any monetary system relies on real-world value.' She was wearing her curls loose and they moved as she spoke. Elsewhere in the room, classical music was being played. 'It is not for no reason,' she continued, 'that the erosion of the gold standard, and other metallist systems, has coincided with unprecedented currency failures, inflationary cycles, and global economic imbalance.'

'Financial crises are more complex than that, and you know it,' the young man snorted.

A short, cynical laugh. Her eyes were fixed on his. 'But, the human psyche is not,' she stated. 'It cannot understand anything less than sight and touch. Commodity money — even tokenised — establishes tangible real-world value.' The young man went to interrupt, but she stopped him with a look. 'Your puny, little mind simply isn't capable of processing anything more complicated than that, James.'

Bristling, the young man, James, snorted again. Opposite, a slow smile spread across his companion's face. Beyond them, dynamic action and a violin suddenly increased in volume. James cleared his throat. 'If currency has a consensual value,' he said, assuredly and unwilling to be defeated, 'then it doesn't need to be backed by anything.' He paused momentarily, examining the expression on the young woman's face. 'Trust. That is the true medium of exchange.'

'Ah,' she grinned, 'but what happens when trust fails? For when that collapses, so does the curr—'

'Nonsense.'

'Unless it is backed by something real,' she narrowed her eyes, 'something to fall back on, something that you can see and touch and understand the value of in terms of purchasing power, then it will collapse. For example—' she raised a finger so as to encourage him to remain quiet. 'For example, James, you can tell me that you have an enormous cock. But—' she paused to allow a smile, slow and twisting, to occupy her lips. When she spoke again, her voice was soft and whispering: 'But, if I don't trust you, then...'

James leant forward, snatching her finger in his hand. 'Well,' he said, smirking and moving closer still, 'I could always show you.'

Immediate scornful laughter. She pulled her finger from his hand. 'And thus you understand the importance of metal-backed currency.' A final smirk and, tossing her curls over her shoulder as she did, she walked away.

The room was filled with people. Musicians, physicians, teachers, *leachers.* Sleeves of her dress fluttering, Mary side-stepped two middle-aged women locked in lively discussion. *Cheese, and who red-napkinned who.* Assigned, consensual value with little to no real-world value, she regarded many of the party's attendants as unnecessary as the conversations they recycled each year.

'Did you find him, Daddy?'

Turning as she approached, her father was standing with Robert and Sophie.

'Edmund,' Mary continued, moving so as to join him at his side. She looped her arm through his.

Comprehension and a smile coloured Ern's face. 'Ah, yes, quite,' he nodded.

'I think he's with Alex, dear.' It was Sophie. Smiling at Mary, she gestured across the room to one of the windows. Black bow tie and cufflinks, Alexander was standing in front of it, nodding as a man with black-grey hair and a half-empty wine glass spoke to him. Mary turned back to her father.

'I spoke with James,' she said to him, nodding as she did. Attentive, spectacled eyes, and she received a slower, less certain nod in return. 'Cleon,' she elaborated, sighing.

Laughter from her father. 'Oh, of course, Cleon! What about?'

'His thesis,' Mary replied. 'It's awful.'

Ern chuckled. 'How so, my love?'

Mary kept her arm looped through his. 'His ideas are poorly-formed,' she explained. 'Myopic. He seems to worship modernisation with ultracrepidarian fervour.' A shake of the head and she softly leant against her father's arm. 'You shall have to speak with him if you expect to get anything useful from him by the end of the academic year.'

Ern was laughing. Opposite, watching their exchange, Robert smiled. 'Having trouble with a student, old friend?' he asked.

Turning to him, Ern nodded jovially. 'So it seems,' he chuckled, straightening his glasses as he did. A grin and he added, 'Monetary economics.'

Eyes moving from her father to Robert, Mary's expression was sour. 'He fancies himself the Governor of the Bank of England or some equivalent delusion.'

Robert gave a laugh. Looking from his daughter to his friend, Ern nodded in confirmation. 'He is quite the egotist,' he chuckled. 'But—' another, louder laugh, and he said, 'that could very well secure him the job!' Both Robert and Ern burst into laughter. Holding hands with her husband, Sophie was smiling. As it was, James was one of Ern's doctoral students, and Mary, often at her father's side, was his cardinal aide and arbiter. Such ensured an impossible task for any student wanting to impress their professor.

'There you are, Ern!' A warm, wide smile, Edmund Goffin had finished talking with Alexander and was now striding across the room towards them. Ern, releasing his daughter, stepped forward so as to shake his hand.

'Wonderful to see you, Eddie!' he exclaimed. 'And,' beaming,

Ern placed his other hand on his friend's elbow, 'congratulations — again — in regards to all your good news!'

Edmund was grinning. 'Thank you, thank you.' A gleeful nod of the head and he patted Ern on the arm. 'Means a lot.' Still grinning, he quickly glanced out across the room, green eyes eager to find the two happy, young couples standing with his wife. Only a few minutes before, Robert — in his customary New Year's Eve address — had announced the fresh engagement of his youngest daughter, Rebecca, to the room. On top of that, his eldest, Lucy, had welcomed her and her husband's first child over the summer.

'So,' Robert said, grinning at Edmund as the group reformed itself, 'a grandfather now.'

Standing next to him, Edmund laughed. 'Yes! Indeed!' More laughter and he looked from Robert to Ern. 'Does that make us old?'

All three men laughed at that. Sophie, still hand-in-hand with Robert, was giggling. Watching them, Mary smiled. Scrunched noses and unceasing, spirited laughter. Seeing them like that made her happy. Gladdened, she found her eyes drawn back across the room to the window. He was standing by himself. Mobile phone in hand, he looked thoroughly and depressingly depressed.

'How goes it, *mec*?' Even from afar, Mary could hear the cheery, accented words of the man who approached the area in front of the window. She watched Alexander stuff his phone into his jacket pocket so as to greet him.

Blue eyes, wavy blonde hair, and trousers the same colour as his shirt, the man's name was Étienne Saint-Clair. The grandson of Sophie's maternal uncle, he had travelled from

France so as to attend the Wheatleighs' annual New Year's party and was, as had been made abundantly clear through the conversations she had heard, in want of a wife.

'He's very handsome, isn't he, marshmallow?'

Mary twisted her head. 'Pardon?'

Smiling pinkly, Sophie had turned from the conversation being had by Ern, Robert and Edmund, and was now looking out across the room with Mary. 'Étienne,' the older woman said, voice light and giggling. 'He's very handsome.'

Mary's eyes returned to the window. Immaculately-groomed, hair purposefully-tousled, arm wrapped around his cousin's shoulder, Étienne was laughing. Alexander, less well-groomed, but woebegone appearance departed, was laughing also.

'You're next to each other on the seating plan.'

Mary turned back to Sophie. 'Étienne?'

A hum and Alexander's mother nodded. Her smile was still pink, and she was clearly very happy.

*Next to each other on the seating plan.* She said it as though she had no control over it. *As though someone other than her had designed it.* A reciprocal hum and, eyes narrowing, Mary looked away from Sophie's soft, joyful face and back towards the two young men by the window. Blue eyes and brown. *The wife-hunter and the—* Mary's thoughts collapsed. She shook her head. *The I-don't-know-quite-what.* Eyes still on the other side of the room, she took a breath. It was going to be a long night.

***

She hadn't chosen to wear red for any particular reason. She had once been told it was a colour that suited her well, no doubt because of her hair and how it — *dark red, at least* — contrasted the fairness of her complexion, but no such thought process had dictated her choice that evening. Rather, newly purchased, spotted in the shop window of a boutique the day before she left for the island, she had thought she might wear the dress for some other occasion. Sophie's birthday was only two weeks away, and she — perfumed with toenails painted — always liked for them to dress up, if only for them then to sit around, watching a film, fire on, cake dispersed, together in the sitting room. And so, her suitcase open on the bed, not yet fully unpacked after her and her father's Christmas Eve arrival, Mary had chosen between the red and a pale blue princess with a delicate illusion neckline and lacey sleeves. Sophie would prefer the blue. It was prettier — *more floaty* — and so she had put on the red. Now, however, walking to find her seat at the dinner table, red velvet all the way to her toes and neck long and exposed, Mary worried that her choice of outfit expressed something. *Something I'd rather it didn't.* A demand for attention. Romantic availability. *Passion.* It was uncomfortable. She wished she had chosen the blue.

The guests scheduled to sit next to her had not yet arrived at their seats and so she found herself momentarily — *gratefully* — alone. Carefully pulling out her chair, she tucked herself and her long, red dress under the table before pushing her curls behind her ears.

*This is going to be awful.*

She quickly glanced the length and breadth of the table.

*More awful than usual.*

Regurgitated platitudes and stale discourse, there would, at least, be *crème brûlée* for dessert.

Minutes passed and more and more guests slowly began to wander in from the other room to take their seats. At the head of the table, Sophie was smiling as she directed people to name cards, hurrying to help when several were knocked over, and Robert and her father were holding onto each other's arms, laughing, loudly, as they always seemed to be, before releasing each other so as to find their own places. The old man was down the other end, quiet, unusually so, with fists clenched on the table in front of him. He caught Mary looking at him and so she offered him a small smile. A simple nod in return then she sat back in her chair, eyes straight ahead, unfocused, waiting for the dinner bell.

'My dining companion for the evening.'

She turned her head and forced a smile. Blue eyes, wavy blonde hair and— *why is he wearing white trousers?* Étienne — *sleeves also rolled up* — returned her smile as he took the seat next to hers.

'I see you are not one for dress codes,' Mary said to him as he sat. Her tone was disapproving, but she maintained her smile and so he laughed.

'Ah,' Étienne chuckled, 'you are the first to say this to me.' He was cheerful and smiled at her. 'But, not, I am certain, the first to think it!'

Black tie typically meant black tie, and Étienne was wearing neither a tie nor anything black.

'I did not realise until under way.'

He was still talking and so she returned to looking at him.

Forward in his chair, touching the cotton napkin arranged on his plate, he was smiling at her. 'Leaving port,' he continued, nodding, 'I remembered the black tie.'

'A shame,' Mary said. More nodding and Étienne's smile widened. A reciprocal smile and she added, voice low, 'I rather thought you'd done it on purpose.'

He laughed at that. *It wasn't a joke.* After all, if he had selected his relaxed, white-trousered, *sans tie* appearance on purpose, he would have proved himself seventy-percent more interesting than most of the other people in the room.

*You shall have to make an effort to be nice to him.*

An inward scoff and Mary reached for her wine glass. It had just been filled and so she took a sip.

*Sophie sat him next to you for a reason.*

Giggling as she walked around the table, ushering Aurélie over to where the other children were seated, Alexander's mother was as lovely and loving as ever. She paused to squeeze her son's shoulder as she passed him. The last thing Mary wanted to do was upset her.

The awkward thing was, Sophie's reason was matrimony. It was not an act of arrogance or unjustified pomposity for Mary to acknowledge that she was the most eligible young woman in the room. *It is the truth.* The heir to one of the Four Families — *but unfortunately female* — she was destined to transfer her father's considerable wealth and status to whichever man was lucky enough to espouse her. Add to that her romantic availability, *not to mention naturally sunny disposition,* and it was no surprise that Étienne Saint-Clair, also an heir — *not of the Founders* — also romantically available, had been seated next to her. Not only that, Mary was quite sure Sophie was worried about her: by putting her and Étienne together, she was giving her a chance.

The first course had entered the room. Silver platters and milk-fed flesh, everyone was happy about it.

Mary unfolded her napkin and draped it across her knees.

'Would you like me to cut you a slice?'

She turned to Étienne. He was smiling and gesturing towards the food. Half-carved on its platter, the knife was currently unattended. A breath and Sophie's soft, joyful face came to mind. Mary looked from Étienne to the meat. *I suppose you can*, and so, 'Yes, please,' she said, sweetly, nodding. More smiling and, reaching for the knife, Étienne appeared very pleased.

Sophie had never meddled before. *Well,* Mary thought, directing a piece of the meat Étienne had cut for her onto the tines of her fork, *asides from with Alex*. But, everyone, so it seemed, had meddled in that, and so that hardly counted anymore. Indeed, one year, possessed by frustration, Alexander had lost his temper, raging at his mother — *and everyone else who happened to be within earshot* — the evening before New Year's Eve about how he would no longer tolerate her seating plan. *No longer tolerate sitting with me.* Every year before, she and Alexander had been neighbours, first at the children's table and then, graduating, together, up to the adults' one. At the age of seventeen, he was finally done, and so he blew his top. It didn't happen very often, but when it did it was always memorable. It had taken Robert some time to soothe Sophie's tears afterwards. Regardless, Alexander got his way: he never sat next to Mary at New Year's again.

*But she's never meddled other than that.*

Forced to observe them both be miserable, Sophie had no doubt hoped Mary and Alexander would find a resolution — either together or separately. After all, she had never been as strongly wedded to the plan as Mary and Alexander's fathers. She, as she had expressed to Mary — both directly and indirectly — only ever hoped for happiness.

*And so she thinks Étienne could mean happiness.*

Chewing on her food, Mary glanced at the man sitting next to her. Knife and fork in hand, he was listening to a conversation taking place further down the table. Someone said something funny and he laughed. It was a pleasant sound — easy, genuinely happy. Mary returned to looking at her plate. The elderberry *jus* was delicious and she wondered if she was easy and genuinely happy too. A thought began to bloom, but just as it did the sound of choking came from the other side of the table. Looking up from her plate, Mary saw that it was Alexander. Sudden and spluttering, something — a piece of bread or baby — must have gone down the wrong way. With tears in his eyes, he struggled to reach for his glass as the woman sitting next to him asked if he was okay.

'Are you enjoying the food, Mary?'

Her eyes moved back to Étienne. Turned in his seat, smiling, he had pronounced her name *à la française. Stressed.* As though there was a second 'r'. *Marie. Marry.* She wasn't sure if she liked it.

'Yes,' Mary said. 'Very much. And you?'

Still smiling, Étienne nodded. 'Very much,' he replied, mirroring her. She reshaped her lips as was appropriate. Meanwhile, on the other side of the table, Alexander had managed to suppress his choking.

'*La gastronomie*,' Étienne continued after a pause to eat, 'it is very important to me.' Again looking at him, Mary nodded. Smiling, he took that as a sign to continue. 'On *L'Étoile*, however,' he had his cutlery in hand, 'good eating is not always possible.'

*L'Étoile*, teak-decked and cream-sailed, was Étienne's sailing yacht. A man of the sea, he had journeyed across the Channel aboard it so as to visit for New Year's. Already showcased to Mary, her father, and the Wheatleighs, the undoubtedly glamorous vessel was now docked on the island's seldom-used jetty, pristine, illuminated by the blue underwater LED lights that ran from bow to stern.

Étienne was still talking. 'I have the galley, of course,' he said, laughing, 'but not always the time. The adventuring,' eyes on hers, he was full of life, 'it can make one forget about all else.'

A small clear of the throat and Mary, setting down her cutlery, turned so as to reach for her wine glass.

'But this—' back to him, he nudged the flesh on his plate with his knife, 'the *terroir* — I can taste the sea air.' He was grinning and so Mary, holding her glass to her lips, offered a smile and nodded. More nodding, more smiling and he pushed the meat onto his fork. He looked at her before raising it to his mouth. 'It reminds me,' he smiled, 'that the adventuring is not everything.'

Food now occupying his mouth, Mary felt the requirement to speak. Returning her glass to the table, she searched for a question. After a moment's consideration: 'What else do you enjoy?' Face soft, she made sure to smile as she waited for him to finish chewing.

Étienne, beaming, swallowed. 'Ah—' a smile and he dabbed his mouth with his napkin, 'many things, many things.' More napkin dabbing and he took a quick sip of wine. 'Hiking, for one. Then, there is climbing, swimming. Also, of course, I like the—' he was struggling and so stopped. Looking at her, a short, uncertain laugh then he extended his arms either side of him, wobbling them up and down, his head bobbing slightly as he did.

Back turned in her chair, watching him, Mary gave a laugh. 'Surfing,' she said with a smile.

Moving his arms back to his sides, Étienne started laughing. 'Of course, *le surf*—' more laughter. 'It is the same! Good!'

Back straight, Mary was still smiling. 'You surf in Normandy?' she asked.

'Sometimes,' he replied, taking another quick drink from his glass. 'The water is cold most of the year, but I have the—' More struggling, he laughed again, embarrassment seeping. '*La combinaison*.'

Mary smiled and nodded. 'You have a wetsuit,' she offered.

Grinning now, Étienne nodded. 'Yes. Thank you.' A further nod and he smiled at her with his eyes. In front of them, both of their plates were empty. Mary reached for her glass again, holding it close to her mouth as Étienne readjusted himself in his chair. 'Your French is very good,' he said to her. '*Oui?*' He watched her take a drink, the sleeves of his shirt pushed up, the front of his hair wavy and stylish.

*Say 'yes' instead of 'no'.*

'Yes,' Mary said. And then, laughing a little, '*Oui*.' Still holding her glass, she smiled at him and explained, '*J'ai appris quand j'étais jeune*.'

He was pleased by that and so responded likewise, in French, telling her how he and his siblings had been taught English together by one of their rather eccentric, tea-drinking tutors. Paying attention to his excited expressions and gesticulations, Mary didn't think it was a good time to tell him that she had learnt French alongside Alexander — at first fast friends and then awkwardly companionable coworkers — and so she kept quiet, happy to listen instead.

Soon after that the first course was cleared away. A brief burst of conversation, then the second appeared. Succulent meat; indulgently golden, dripping-roasted potatoes; aromatic bread stuffing; and flavoursome, buttered vegetables. Étienne offered once again to serve her food for her; this time she agreed without hesitation.

In between mouthfuls of food, he spoke to her about sailing, about his time in French Polynesia — *le meilleur endroit pour surfer, Marie* — and about his love for spearfishing. He asked her questions too, being sure to stop and enquire whenever the conversation leant that way, shuffling closer to her each time that he did so as to be able to hear her over the sound of the rest of the table. Had she ever visited French Polynesia? Would she one day like to? They were simple questions with simple answers, and yet she couldn't help but think that — simply by entertaining them — she was offending someone.

And yet, as he served himself a second helping of julienne parsnips, smiling as she told him, '*non, je n'ai pas*', but that she had spent a summer in California, where there was also surfing, the year her father had lectured at an international economics forum, she realised that it felt good to have someone express, what appeared to be at least, genuine interest in her life.

He was telling her about the custom rigging he had commissioned for *L'Étoile* now. Slicing a slither of meat, Mary nodded to let him know that she was listening.

*It isn't perfect.*

Another nod and she raised her fork to her mouth.

*But maybe one day it could be.*

Despite appearances, Mary was a very sensitive person. Soft underneath it all, sentimental, romantic, even, she had a deep yearning to be loved. Her father, a widower of thirteen years who had not once entertained the idea of remarriage after her mother died, had taught her that love was everything. It could easily destroy a person, but that was only because, when given and enjoyed, it was like nothing else. Mary wanted to know what that felt like. *Really feels like.* Having recently turned twenty years of age, she was long past fairy stories and imaginative tales of chivalric knight-errants rescuing tower-trapped princesses.

*And yet here he is.* More talk of rigging and she smiled at Étienne. *A white knight aboard a sailed steed.*

But, as she had already concluded, it wasn't perfect. And yet, time was moving — and she wasn't.

Mary reached for her glass and took a sip. Noticing that it was almost empty, Étienne — putting down his knife and fork — immediately intervened. Quiet in her chair, she smiled as she watched him refill it for her.

Indeed, when considered, the young man at her side ticked many boxes. He was charming and capable, wealthy and well-educated. *Not of the Founders*, but certainly — as the heir to the

Saint-Clair family — second best. *And*, as Sophie had pointed out earlier in the evening, *he is very handsome*. Not only that, he — passing her glass back to her with a soft smile — gave her something that no one else had ever given her — *the chance to be a normal person*. She wouldn't get a better offer.

'Excuse me.'

Sudden movement on the other side of the table. Alexander had just stood up. The course, let alone the meal, not yet concluded, he abandoned his napkin on his chair, a cast-off of crumpled cotton, and strode towards the door and out of the room. Silence swelled in his wake. His mother's head turned as if to follow him. Next to her, Robert, eyes also on their son, touched the back of her hand to stop her. Seats away, glass in hand, Mary exhaled as she watched the door close behind him.

*What is wrong with you?* she thought, voice exasperated, even in her head.

Another exhale, this time softer, and she turned back to Étienne. Eager blue eyes, wavy, blonde hair, and a smile just for her. *I won't get a better offer*. Giving him a smile in return, Mary set her glass down on the table before tucking her curls back behind her ears.

'I like the colour of your hair,' Étienne said to her, happy, easy. '*Très jolie*.'

Mary, still smiling, nodded and thanked him.

The more they talked, the clearer it became to Mary that — if she truly wanted it — her life could look entirely different in a year's time. She could be married. Have a child on the way. *Be in French Polynesia*. It was remarkable, the difference that twelve months could make. She could have everything she ever wanted — *love, a future, a family of my own.* Of course, that would mean abandoning, *at least in part*, the family she already had. Her father, Sophie, Robert, Guinevere, Aurélie, the old man. *Alexander.*

She hated that it always came back to him. Scraping the last of her vegetables onto her fork, Mary looked out across the table towards his empty chair. He was gone, *but never really.* Maybe Étienne could be the arrow through the heart that she needed: a way to give herself permission to pursue genuine happiness, to give herself to someone, someone who would love her each and every day, *and not once upon a dream a very long time ago.*

'*Tu vas bien, Marie?*'

She turned back to Étienne. 'Yes.' A smile. 'Sorry,' she apologised. 'My thoughts were elsewhere for a moment.'

Smiling, charming, he didn't seem to mind, and instead ushered her towards a new topic of conversation. Her favourite book? He had read, and enjoyed, the same author only the year before. It was pleasant to have something in common. How about her favourite film? That, too, he had seen. And so there were commonalities galore.

By the time the *crème brûlée* was served, she had had her fill of sweetness. The chair on the other side of the table still empty, she was feeling slightly affected by the wine, her glass not having been allowed to be empty at any point during the meal. More talk of sailing. *Rigging. Marie. Marry.* She was anxious for the fireworks. Fresh air. *That's what I need.* To clear her head. *To think about this.* In here, next to happy, easy Étienne, she felt as though she were suffocating.

She was able to sneak away to the bathroom before they

went outside. A moment to splash water on her cheeks and remind herself that she was okay, then she went back downstairs, smiling, ready to watch the fireworks on the driveway.

He was already outside. Slumped. Sitting on the steps beside the front door, there was an empty bottle of wine not too far away. Everyone else, chatting and cheerful, ignored him as they flowed through the door and down the steps onto the gravel. Étienne was standing with her father. She saw that they were talking as she approached from the house.

'Are you okay, my love?' Ern asked with a smile as she moved to stand next to him.

A nod and Mary mirrored his expression. Étienne, not saying anything, but smiling also, repositioned himself so that he was at her side.

The fireworks were spectacular. Woven clusters of gold, erupting, like stars from a nebula, spraying glittering trails of light across the night. Another boom, and a comet of green replaced the gold, mapping the open sky before dividing, dramatically, into five separate, sparkling explosions. Then, crackling, and the stars fell, gently drifting to Earth before being covered up by yet another boom. There was sulphur in the air, and Mary watched it all unfold above her — the scarring of the sky — as everyone announced the New Year.

'You are shivering, Marie.'

She turned her head from the stars. Étienne was looking at her.

'Oh,' she said, glancing down at her arm. Exposed skin, goosebumps. *Shaking.* 'Yes,' she nodded, turning back to look at him. 'I am.'

He smiled at that, offering to get her something to keep

her warm. He was already gone, striding back towards the house, before she had a chance to stop him, and so she returned to watching the fireworks.

'Wonderful young man.'

Mary turned her head again.

'Very interesting.' Her father had his eyes on the sky as he spoke to her. 'Did you know,' he said, raising his voice a little as yet more colours exploded above them, 'that he had a chance to observe traditional dance in Tahiti — *'ori Tahiti.*'

Mary shook her head. 'No, I didn't.'

Ern turned to look at her now. 'Fascinating stuff,' he chuckled. 'Spiritual. Very energetic.' Another chuckle and — booming cascades of colour — he turned back to the fireworks. 'Not quite sure why he was so eager to talk to me about it.'

Mary, eyes still on her father, took a long, slow breath. 'It's almost like he wants something,' she said dryly.

Her father laughed at that, the sound very almost as loud as the fireworks. 'A boat, head full of hair, heir to a fortune—' smiling through his glasses, he looked down at her. 'What more could he possibly want?

Another long, slow breath and Mary shook her head.

Étienne was walking back to them. He was holding a blanket. 'How is this?' he asked, offering it to Mary once he was close enough for her to hear him. He was smiling and so she nodded. Stepping forward, draping it over her shoulders, tucking it around her neck, his hands brushed against her skin as he covered her. A twisting, tingling sensation that ran from her neck, down the length of her spine and straight into her stomach, Mary felt sick. Shaking still, she hurried to look back at the fireworks.

*I'm worried.*

Focusing on a coil of bright red light, her eyes were going fuzzy.

*Worried this isn't what I want.*

A breath.

*Worried, also, that it might be.*

Adjusting the blanket so that it was wrapped more tightly around her torso, she held onto herself and prayed for the shaking to stop.

In the end, she announced that she needed to use the bathroom again. A nod from her father and Étienne, his trail of light persistent and bright, offered to walk her inside the house.

'You don't have to,' she said. Head shaking. He was more than happy to do so, and so, smiling, arms falling to her sides, she began to cross the gravel to the front door with him. He was talking about his boat again, and about how she might like him to take her out sailing tomorrow.

'Mary!'

Robert Senior was standing by the front door, supporting himself on his walking cane as he gestured to her. His grandson was at his feet, still slumped, still sitting on the step, his head in his hands.

'Mary,' the old man said again, 'are you going inside?'

Nodding, she climbed the steps towards him. Étienne followed.

'Be a good girl,' Alexander's grandfather continued, 'and fetch me another glass of whisky. My knee—' a moment to shuffle against his cane and he winced, 'it's being a right old bugger in this cold.'

Mary smiled at him. 'Alright, old man. But,' her voice was soft, 'you really should go inside if it's causing that much pain.'

Unconcerned, Robert Senior wafted his hand. Another smile and she turned towards the door, Étienne close behind.

'No, Mary—' the old man was still looking at her. 'Make sure it's the good stuff.' Arms folded, holding the blanket to her chest, Mary turned to listen. 'The old crystal decanter, with the dodgy stopper,' Robert Senior continued. He was nodding enthusiastically as he spoke. Alexander, meanwhile, head still in his hands, was unmoving. 'I got your father to pull it from the cabinet and hide it in the cupboard in the hallway,' the old man explained. 'Right at the back — you might have to dig around for it. Didn't want any of these wastrels—' lifting his cane, he waved it towards the people on the driveway, 'pilfering the whisky cabinet when I wasn't looking.'

Mary laughed at that. Curls jiggling as she shook her head, she looked between the cheery, chattering guests on the gravel and the complaining old man. At his grandfather's feet, Alexander lifted his head from his hands. A miserable, drowning expression, he momentarily caught Mary's eye.

*What is wrong with you?* she thought, the voice in her head softer this time.

Shifting on his walking cane, Robert Senior was talking to Étienne now. A devilish smile and he asked him whether or not he was a whisky man.

Standing on one of the steps in front of Alexander, Étienne smiled. 'No, I am afraid not,' he answered.

Robert Senior laughed. 'I would have thought it right up your alley, captain of your little boat as you are. A nice glass of whisky, or brandy—' Alexander's grandfather paused and devil-smile growing, added, 'Cognac?'

Étienne shook his head.

Robert Senior was still smiling. Both Mary and Alexander's eyes moved to follow the exchange. 'A nice glass of whisky,' the old man continued, 'sailing into port, a couple of beautiful women on deck.'

Étienne started laughing. Arms easy at his side, he grinned at the older man. 'You sound like an old sailor, Dr. Wheatleigh. But with *l'Étoile* and I,' his grin got wider, 'it is not like that.'

The old man chuckled. 'Oh really,' he said, readjusting himself on his walking cane. 'What is it like, then? I thought the main benefit of owning a yacht was its ability to attract the fairer sex.'

Mary, watching Étienne laugh again, wondered whether the old man was being hostile or hospitable.

'It is for the sport, Dr. Wheatleigh,' Étienne smiled, gesticulating, easily, happily, as he replied to Alexander's grandfather. 'The adventure, also.' The young man continued to explain his passion, describing the wind and the sails — *the rigging, Marie, marry* — and Mary noticed Alexander was staring down at the step on which his cousin was standing.

*Perhaps he isn't feeling very well.*

As if hearing her, Alexander raised his head.

*He hasn't been okay since he came home.*

Étienne was still illuminating Robert Senior. 'It is as though you are the only person to exist,' he smiled.

Alexander, hands over his stomach, looked down again.

*Maybe that's why he was coughing at the table.* Mary's eyes moved between Alexander's empty glass and the empty wine bottle. *Or, some other reason.*

'I was saying to Marie,' eagerness, Étienne briefly turned to look at her, 'only a few minutes ago, how energising it is to be out on the sea, to experience the swelling of the waves. For the first time, especially, the big waves most of all—' he paused then, looking at her again. Mary, giving him her attention, nodded and smiled. Opposite, Robert Senior was smirking. 'There is nothing quite like it. I suggested—' a wide, white-toothed smile and Étienne, oblivious to the old man's mockery, was looking at her again, 'that before I leave, I could take her out on *l'Étoile* and—'

The sound of vomit killed his speech. And, unfortunately for Étienne, it wasn't just the sound, but the substance also. An involuntary, forceful, traumatic expulsion — *not unlike the dramatically dividing green comet firework* — Alexander had just been sick all over his cousin's shoes and white trousers.

Choking desperation. 'I'm so sorry.' Cadaverous humiliation. 'I get seasick—'

And then he did it again.

It was horrific. *Hilariously horrific.* The blanket slipping from her shoulders, Mary's hands immediately moved to cover her mouth. At her side, thoroughly shocked, but thoroughly merry, the old man was momentarily transformed to marble. Meanwhile, on the floor, holding himself, flecks of sick caught in the corners of his mouth, Alexander was stuttering. Étienne, standing, vomit-covered, the same.

'I'm so sorry—'

Hands flapping.

'No, no, *mec*—'

Attempts at assistance.

'I never—'

Begging for forgiveness.

'Don't worry yourself, I will go and clean myself.'

Utterly splattered, his shoes and trousers now hideously patterned, Étienne took a step away from Alexander.

Unlike Mary, Robert Senior was moving again. 'It's alright, lad,' he said, words tangled up in laughter. 'Let me get you inside.' With that, he shoved his hand under his grandson's armpit and pulled his soft, shaking body up off the step.

Mary's hands were still over her mouth. Étienne was walking away.

'You'd best help him.' It was Robert Senior. Gripping Alexander, he nodded at the other young man. 'Make sure he gets to his boat okay.'

Mary, slowly returning to the moment, nodded at the old man, her hands dropping from her mouth. As they did, she looked at Alexander. A jolt of desperate, dying eye contact. Vitality, and she felt a grin twist her lips, before forcing herself to turn and catch up to Étienne.

Blonde hair still perfectly tousled, he was striding across the driveway. Mary snatched the blanket he had given to her from the gravel, the skirt of her dress likewise, and hurried after him.

'*Tu vas bien?*' She was trying not to laugh. '*Étienne?*'

At that, he stopped and turned so as to wait for her. Around them, everyone else on the driveway, laughing, chattering, drunk, appeared oblivious.

'Are you okay?' Mary asked again, smoothing the creases of her smile.

Slowly, he nodded.

'Oh my goodness,' she said, catching her breath. 'I barely know what happened.'

Étienne's voice was happy and easy. 'It is New Year's,' he said, smiling at her. 'Sometimes people drink too much.'

Her smile returning, Mary nodded softly. *He isn't perfect.* Happy, easy, perfect blue eyes and happy, easy, perfect blonde hair. *He's too perfect.* She continued to smile at him, thinking only of Alexander's face after he had vomited all over him. *Too perfect.* Seeing her joy, Étienne smiled also. With that, they continued walking together.

His boat illuminated the water beneath it. Beautiful blue LEDs, beautiful mahogany hull, beautiful teak deck, beautiful everything. He invited her to follow him on board, she could sit and have a drink whilst he cleaned himself, after which they would return to the party, but she politely declined, telling him that she would meet him back at the house. And so, shoes squelching as he walked along the jetty, he smiled at her as she turned and left him.

The sky was clear as she walked back to the house. Deep blue, sparkling with stars, the regnant Moon creamy and yellow. Smiling to herself, Mary tightened the blanket around her shoulders. She was cold, but she wasn't shaking anymore. Then, ahead of her on the path, the house but a distant beacon of orange light, she heard something move. Tightening the blanket yet again, she stepped towards the sound.

'Are you following me?'

Grumbling and the rustling of vegetation. 'Might have been,' a voice replied.

A short laugh and Mary extended her hand out in front of her. Moving out from the shadow of a low hedge, hobbling along the path towards her, the old man took it and rested it on the crook of his arm. More laughter and Mary leant against him. Their heads bobbed in rhythm with his walking cane as they slowly resumed the path together.

'So,' she asked, smiling, 'why were you following me?'

Robert Senior gave a snort. 'To make sure that Frenchie didn't invite you onto his yacht.'

Mary laughed. 'Well,' she said, 'he did.'

Another snort from the old man. 'I knew it.'

'No, you didn't,' she retorted, nudging his arm as they walked together. 'I didn't need saving.'

At that, Robert Senior cackled a laugh. Mary, still leaning against him, grinned and looked towards the light of the house. The night was getting colder. A few seconds later, the old man spoke again. His voice was softer than before.

'Don't do what I think you're thinking of doing, Mary.' Still walking, he had turned his head and was looking at her.

A short laugh and Mary smiled. 'I don't know what you're talking about, old man,' she said.

Robert Senior didn't laugh, but stopped instead. Her hand was still in the crook of his arm and he encouraged her to turn to face him. Serious grey eyes, the old man looked at her. 'Settling,' he said. 'Don't do it.' He paused, humourless, searching her. Mary didn't say anything. 'Don't settle for something less than what you want,' Robert Senior continued. Then, with a deep breath, 'It's not right.'

Mary was silent. Motionless in the yellow moonlight of the New Year, she allowed Robert Senior to examine her. Seventy-five years old, he had lost his wife the previous January. This was his first New Year's without her.

A moment or two longer, then he continued chaperoning her back to the house. They walked in silence for the rest of the way, Mary leaning against him, her thumb softly brushing the fabric of his old, black jacket as they did.

'Is he alright?' she asked once they reached the front door.

'You can ask him yourself,' Robert Senior barked, the softness of before gone. He shrugged her off of him then, before struggling up the steps with his walking cane, voice loud as he called, through the door and into the house, for her father. 'That damn whisky,' he complained. 'Putting it right at the back of the cupboard — I don't know what he was thinking!'

Mary couldn't help but laugh as she watched him go. The rest of the party was indoors, in the back room of the house, dancing, as was annual custom. Following Robert Senior inside, she closed the front door behind her, before draping the blanket over the elegant wooden cap at the bottom of the bannister and heading upstairs.

His bedroom door was slightly open, the light inside turned on. She knocked and waited, but there was no reply. Carefully, she pushed on the door and stepped inside.

'Alex?'

Bed empty, his shoes abandoned on the carpet, he wasn't there. Mary could see light leaking out from under his bathroom door and so crossed the carpet towards it. Knuckles soft on the wood, she again knocked and waited.

'Come in.' His voice was low and filled with suffering. Slowly, she pushed on the door and peered inside.

He was sitting on the floor, legs spread apart, head turned miserably in the direction of the open toilet. When he realised it was her, he didn't necessarily look pleased to see her.

'Are you okay?' Mary asked, all but whispering.

He gave a small nod.

Voice still quiet, she asked him if he needed anything. 'I can get you a cold glass of water.'

'I'm okay,' he whispered back. Slowly, he raised his eyes to meet hers. 'Thank you.'

Now it was her turn to nod.

'Is Étienne alright?'

'He'll be okay.'

'I hope I didn't ruin his evening—' his eyes were still on hers, 'or yours.'

'I don't think you did that.'

Nodding from the floor. His eyes, big and brown, were as soft as ever and, *as ever*, encouraged her heart to expand.

A smile, at first soft, then something else, formed on her lips. 'I didn't think he'd ever stop talking about his stupid boat,' she said. Twisting now, her expression morphed to a smirk. 'But, I suppose it was an awful lot of vomit.'

Looking at each other across the room, it was as though there was a landslide. Smiles slipped to sound and they both burst into laughter.

Alexander, eyes closing, shook his head. 'I was shaking!'

Pink joy, Mary's laughter grew alongside his.

His head was in his hands now. 'Oh my God,' he struggled, still laughing, 'did it really happen?'

'That—' giggling, she shook her head, 'That was my thought!'

He was breathless and made a sound of muffled, laughter-laced desperation, causing her to giggle all the more.

'I—' she was clutching her chest, 'when I—'

Looking up at her, Alexander was nodding, grinning.

'Walking to the boat—' she continued, eyes on his, 'his shoes—' more giggling and, with a burst of breath, she managed, 'Squelching!'

'Oh God!' Shameful, crying laughter. 'That's horrible!'

Still standing in the doorway, eyes squeezed shut, she nodded furiously. The sound was rolling now, utterly uncontrolled, and he struggled to keep himself upright. Letting his head rest against the sink cupboard, he grinned up at her as she was likewise unable to compose herself.

'It's like the time with the milk,' he beamed at her, gesturing to his face as he did.

Remembrance, and Mary opened her eyes so as to meet his. 'No—' Chest squeezing and she shook her head. 'It's not at all!'

They fought it after that. Panting, breathless agony, the pain of too much laughter, and they slowly started to quieten. Eventually, the laughter faded.

Mary was smiling at him from the door. 'Are you sure you don't want some water?'

Mirroring her, he shook his head.

'Alright, then.' Eyes soft, she looked at him one last time, then turned to leave. Closing the door behind her, she walked back across his bedroom carpet and out onto the landing.

Stopping herself before she went down the stairs, she took a deep breath.

*What on Earth was that?*

Looking. Speaking. Laughing.

*Everything we never do.*

Thinking back to earlier in the evening — to dinner, to fireworks, to Étienne — Mary knew what she wanted. Another deep breath and she walked down the stairs and along the hallway to the back of the house.

It didn't take him long, fresh pair of white trousers, to reappear. Smiling when he saw her, sat by herself on a chair overlooking the dancefloor, he said her name as he approached.

'Clean?' she asked, tone cheerful.

A laugh and Étienne nodded. He moved to stand in front of her. Blue eyes and blonde hair, crisp white shirt, white trousers, and a pair of canvas shoes the same dark and elegant shade of blue as his jacket. She smiled as she looked at him. *The most perfect second best.*

'Dance with me, Marie?' he asked, extending a hand to her.

Beyond, the music was joyful, the dancers the same.

'I can't,' Mary said, smile unchanged.

A flash of confusion and Étienne laughed. 'Come,' he said, grinning, gesturing to her with his hand. 'I am rather good.'

Smiling still, she slowly shook her head. *I don't doubt that you are, but—* 'I can't,' she said again. 'I'm sorry.'

Another laugh from the man in the white trousers. 'Just one,' he negotiated, voice easy and happy. 'Just a dance. It doesn't have to mean anything.'

At that, Mary laughed. It was a soft, tender sound, one

which evolved from somewhere in the past. 'Oh, Étienne,' she said, smiling at him from the chair, 'that's the thing — it always means something.'

After she said that, there was a moment, a moment to look at each other, before, softly, he said, '*Je comprends.*'

But, he didn't — and there was no way that he could. And so, she let him have it.

'Thank you,' Mary said, nodding.

A slow, sad smile, then he forced the easy happiness back into his voice. '*Bonne année, Marie.*'

'*Bonne année, Étienne.*'

Reaching for her, he took her hand at that and, slowly, brought it to his lips. As their skin contacted, he kept his eyes on hers; soft, and then, with a sudden turn, he left her.

*Happy New Year, white knight.* Mary brought her hands together in her lap and sighed. Before she had a chance to dwell on it, however, there was a laugh, followed by a voice from her right. 'Good,' it scoffed. 'You've sent him packing.' A broad stride and the chair next to her was filled. 'I was wondering when you would get around to that.'

Mary turned to look at the young man sitting next to her. Her eyes immediately narrowed.

Sighing, over-exaggeratedly, he pushed his face close to hers and said, 'Alright then, you've worn me down.' Suddenly, he stood and thrust his hand towards her. 'I'll dance with you.'

Laughing sharply, Mary slapped his hand away. 'Fuck off, James.'

Grinning, grimacing, the young man snorted a laugh. His back was straight and expression priggish. 'I'll see you at university in a couple of weeks then.'

With that she wafted her hand, shooing him. 'I'd rather not.'

More snorting, scoffing laughter and James walked off, away to find another young woman to terrorise. As he moved from view, the rest of the room revealed itself. Happy couples, young and old, Edmund Goffin's daughters, married and soon-to-be; an elderly couple, hands together, swaying much too slowly; and there, in the centre, Robert and Sophie, tired, happy, her head resting against his chest as he held her to him, slowly guiding her back and forth as the music instructed. Sitting in her chair, watching them, Mary smiled. Love could easily destroy a person, *but that's only because it's like nothing else.* It was everything.

Tired, yawning, she stretched her legs out in front of her and, black heels poking from the hem of her dress, decided it was time for bed. Standing up from her chair, she caught her father's eye across the room, nodding at him, mouthing 'goodnight', before walking to the door. Back along the hallway and, hand soft on the handrail, she pulled herself up the stairs to bed.

Alexander's bedroom door was slightly open. Light still on, he was playing music inside. Mellifluous, flowing, it was a song she liked. She took a moment to listen and then, opening the door to her own room, went inside. Light switch on and she turned, eyes out onto the landing, listening, again, to the music coming from the other room. Happy to hear it, she left her own door slightly open too, before slipping off her shoes and climbing, fully clothed, entirely exhausted, into bed.

# The Object of Eternal Pity

*Continuing on from the events of The Homestead's Chapter Four, Mary awaits Alexander's return to the island. Unseen by him, she suffers the arrival of his unexpected guest.*

There was no mistaking the sound. Crunching over gravel and the clunking of metal, the handbrake applied too suddenly, the exhaust pipe old and rusted, juddering, the vibration of the engine causing it to contact the body of the car. He would wait to silence the engine; the key in the ignition had a tendency to stick unless the steering wheel was in the correct position and he never did get it quite right the first time. But, he wouldn't change it. The car might have been old, but it was his, and it worked — just about.

*He is home.*

It had been nine months since she had seen him last.

*A threadbare suitcase and New Year's leftovers.*

He had left too quickly. They should have realised he wasn't going to come home — not for a while, at least. Eyes down, he had crossed her on the stairs — *an omen of ill fortune if you are looking for one* — and neither one of them had said anything.

Upon hearing the car on the driveway, everyone else rushed outside. Sophie was first through the front door. She had been preparing food all day, having saved an especially nice cut of meat from the last harvest just for his return. The old man had wanted to eat it when it was fresh and at its best; Sophie had made sure it ended up in the freezer. Standing at the top of the stairs, just outside the door to her bedroom and opposite the door to his, Mary could smell it — sweet and caramelised, seasoned with fresh herbs — roasting in the oven.

She didn't want to be there when he got out of the car. He didn't want her there. Time had taught her that. Hands tucked into the pockets of her cardigan, she would wait until they ate to say hello to him. Below, the old man was standing in the doorway, looking out of the front door at the driveway. Mary watched from the shadows as he gripped his walking cane. Then, he laughed. It was a sudden, sharp sound and caught her by surprise. Shuffling across the carpet, she looked down the stairs. There was no way to see what was happening outside, *only green tweed and the orange of the lights that led away from the door,* but she knew something wasn't right. It was then that she heard another sound. A voice that wasn't his and wasn't anyone else's. Still holding onto his cane, the old man turned in the doorway to look up the stairs. Grey eyes and he shook his head at her.

Without the lights turned on to illuminate it, the upstairs landing was already dark, but at that moment it became darker still. Pulling her hand from her pocket, she yanked the door to her bedroom, opening it, stumbling through it. Inside, her knees soon found the carpet, the palms of both her hands likewise seeking the soft reassurance of its fibres. Her cheeks were wet and she didn't know why: a long time ago she had told herself that there was no way he could hurt her any more than he already had.

She measured the passing of time against her own breathing. Short at first, then forced to slow, she felt as though she had swallowed the entire room's oxygen by the time he came up the stairs. *Soft, careful footsteps. Socks on the carpet.* Only, it wasn't just him. There were two sets of feet and the voice that mumbled in response to his, barely within Mary's hearing, was one she didn't recognise. Crawling across the floor to the crack at the bottom of the door, she pressed her cheek to the carpet and listened.

'It doesn't matter,' the voice said.

Then, the door to his bedroom was opened and closed and she could hear no more.

Mary sat up against the door. The wood was hard against her back and there was a ladder in her tights. It was ugly to look at. Pushing her finger through it, she made the tear bigger. *It's already broken. What difference does it make?* When the entire left leg of her tights was thoroughly ruined, she kicked them off, pulled herself up off the carpet, and crossed the room to throw them in her bathroom bin. Water splashed on her cheeks to dullen the pain, then she left her bedroom and went downstairs.

The door to the kitchen was closed. Slipping through it, she was careful to shut it again without making too much noise. On the other side of the room, Alexander's mother was leaning over the worktop, hands firmly planted on the surface either side of an empty serving dish. She jumped when she realised someone was in the room with her, one hand rushing to her bosom, the other to her mouth. When she turned and saw it was Mary, her surprise, and hands, melted away, leaving nothing but desolation in their place.

'My marshmallow,' Sophie said, her voice wobbling as she whispered across the room. 'I—' she caught herself and swallowed. 'Were you upstairs?'

Folding her arms across her chest, Mary leant against the old oak sideboard next to the door. 'I came to see if you need any help,' she replied.

Sophie said she didn't and, voice soft and slow, asked if she was alright.

'I'm fine,' Mary said without expression. Everyone knew that she loved him, *and that's always what makes it worse.*

'I can get Robert—' once again Sophie trailed off. She tucked her hair behind her ears before continuing. 'To speak with him.'

Mary shook her head. 'Please,' she said, scarcely above a whisper.

Sophie's lips quivered as if she were about to say something more. She didn't, simply nodding instead. On the worktop beside the range cooker, the egg timer rang. Sophie reached for the oven gloves and moved towards it. Watching her as she did, Mary loosened her arms from her chest. 'When the food's ready,' she said, 'I'll take mine down to the Seat.'

Sophie abandoned the oven. 'No, dear—' a shake of her head and she crossed the room to reach her. 'No, dear. You can't eat by yourself.' Oven gloves still on her hands, she pulled the younger woman into an embrace. Stiffening in her arms, Mary conjured thoughts of snow and ice, grasping the cold so as to quell the heat of her emotion. *There is no way it can hurt any more.*

'Please,' Sophie cried, 'I don't want you to.' Her breath was warm on Mary's ear and the sorrow in her voice tempted the tears to return. More snow. More ice. 'This is your home,' Sophie continued. The syllables were elongated and it sounded like she was crying. Sophie pulled away and met the eyes of the other woman. 'Let me get Robert—'

'Sophie, please—'

'Let me get him.'

Removing the oven gloves from her hands, she discarded them on the sideboard and exited the kitchen, leaving the door slightly ajar. Mary worried that he would be on the other side, but he wasn't. The hallway was empty, the rest of the household elsewhere. Earlier, she had heard the back door slam as Alexander's grandfather had left to return to his little cottage at the back of the house. It opened now, guided by a softer pair of hands, inviting a breeze inside. A low voice hummed down the hallway. Arms back across her chest, Mary stared at the floor and waited for Robert and Sophie to reach the open kitchen door.

'Tell her she can't eat by herself, Robert.'

Entering the kitchen, Robert closed the door behind them.

'It simply isn't right.'

'I don't know what you expect me to say.' Robert's brow was furrowed. The lines disappeared when he caught Mary looking at him. He offered her a smile, but it looked more sad than anything else. *The object of eternal pity.*

'Dinner will be ruined,' Sophie said, visibly pleading with her husband as she stood in front of him, eyes flickering between him and Mary.

He sighed. 'I think it may already be, my darling.' Placing a hand on her arm, he caressed her. They were both whispering and yet each word was delivered with the same strength of emotion as if they were speaking at normal volume.

Sophie reached for the oven gloves and returned to the cooker. The carrots had started to burn.

'Let me,' Robert offered, crossing the room as smoke swelled from the open door. Taking the gloves from her, he lifted the roasting tin onto the stove. 'I'll drive you down,' he said next, turning his head to look at Mary over his shoulder.

'Robert—'

'It's okay, my darling,' Robert interrupted his wife. A breath and he touched her arm again. 'We can fix it in the morning.'

But, there was nothing to fix. It was simply the way that it was, *and the way that it is meant to be.* Tomorrow would be just another day and what would come would come. Eventually, they would all end up where they were meant to be, but, until then, they had to suffer the present. *At this point, it's the only thing left to believe.*

'Would you like me to cut the roast?' Robert asked his wife, smiling at her in an attempt to ease her distress.

Sophie nodded. 'It needs another ten minutes.'

'Okay,' Robert smiled, 'another ten minutes, then.'

Mary was still leaning against the sideboard and she spoke now, 'Do you still need me tomorrow evening?'

Robert looked across at her. 'The dry fresher?' he asked.

Mary nodded.

A sigh. 'Unfortunately, yes.' He shook his head and moved across the room to be closer to her. 'There's no other option.'

Again, Mary nodded.

'Frank and I can manage if you—'

'No.' Mary shook her head and forced a smile. 'It's fine, you know I'll help.'

Robert nodded. Across the room, Sophie was once more at the range cooker. She asked Robert to pass her another plate from the cupboard — the seven he had arranged on the table earlier in the day now no longer enough — and so he got one and brought it to her.

'All the vegetables, dear?' Sophie asked, turning to catch Mary's eye.

She nodded.

Sophie spooned a portion of carrots onto the plate. She had pulled another roasting tin from the top oven and moved to that next. As she served Mary's meal, the three of them were silent, Sophie at the range cooker, Mary against the sideboard, and Robert with his eyes on the window. Outside, it was getting dark earlier than usual. The season was changing.

'You can do the roast now, dear.'

Robert nodded and moved to the cooker. The knife was sharp and the slices were carved with surgical precision; and so the meat which Sophie had saved for her son's return would already be cut by the time it reached the table.

'Put some foil over it — by the bread bin, dear—' Sophie wafted her hand at Mary, 'so it doesn't get cold on the way down.' Once the foil was over the plate, Mary thanked her for the food. Robert was waiting by the door.

'You don't need to thank me, marshmallow,' Sophie said softly and reached to tweak her nose. 'Please come back up after you've finished.'

'I will,' Mary said. Then, plate in hand, she moved to the door. Robert held it open for her and they left the house together.

They were both quiet at first. It was colder than either one of them had expected and Mary felt herself shivering as she held the plate, foil crinkling against her cardigan as she pressed it against her in an attempt to syphon any of the heat that was able to escape.

'It's just a fad.'

Mary sniffed and raised her eyes from the plate.

'A short-lived act of rebellion,' Robert continued, his hands on the steering wheel as he guided the farm buggy down the hill. 'A way for him to convince himself of something he already knows.'

Mary tightened her embrace of the plate. 'He seems awfully invested in this short-lived experiment.'

Robert hummed. On the other side of the windscreen, the habitation buildings were coming into view. 'Some of us simply need more time to digest how we feel,' he replied. He glanced across the buggy then, smiling at her. 'That's all.'

Mary attempted a nod.

They were there now, at the homestead's central office, an old stone building that contained the camera displays and override controls to all the electronic locks on the island. They called it the Seat. Robert slowed the buggy to a halt.

'You'll do as you said—' Robert turned from the steering

wheel to look at her, 'come back up after you've finished eating?'

Mary readjusted the plate in her hands and began to climb out of the buggy. 'Eventually,' she said. Slipping a hand under her cardigan, she retrieved the brass key she wore around her neck as a pendant and walked towards the Seat. 'I'd rather not have to listen to him—' Mary paused and looked at Robert, 'digest his feelings.'

Robert didn't say anything, only sighed.

'Thank you for driving me down,' Mary added, her voice softer than before.

Robert nodded. Straightening his trousers, he went to stand. 'I'll leave you the buggy,' he said.

Mary shook her head. 'You take it,' she replied. 'I'll walk back when I'm finished.

'Are you sure?'

She nodded. A moment and then:

'Very well, then.'

A final look at each other and she turned and followed the path to the door. Robert watched her enter the building before he drove away.

Inside the Seat, the monitors were off. Mary set the plate Sophie had given to her down on the desk in front of them. A push of a button and the screens illuminated. She switched to the camera positioned in front of the main house. Alexander's little red car was still in the driveway.

*I know you*, Mary thought. And so she knew — she prayed — this wasn't him.

# The First Night

*It is the evening after The Homestead's Chapters Six and Seven — and thus the evening after Tammy and Alexander's relationship ended. Mary is in her room, preparing for bed.*

A tealight under the burner and a few drops of ylang-ylang essential oil in the water. Heady and fragrant, the scent seemed to wrap itself around the air in the room, draping the space in a floral embrace. Seated at her dressing table in her pyjamas, Mary was detangling her curls, a bottle of hair oil open in front of her. She was careful to separate them into segments, stopping to smooth the ends through her fingers as she did. Next to her, the flame of the candle flickered as someone opened a door outside in the hallway, the draft pushing itself into her bedroom.

The knock on her door took her by surprise. It was quiet and unsure, a faster knock splintered mid-beat to become a softer one. A sound that melted as it was created. Fastening the bottle of oil, Mary rose from the dressing table and moved to the door.

He asked if he could come in and she, confused and not knowing what to say, nodded and allowed it. Closing the door behind him, she caught sight of herself in the mirror of the dressing table. She suddenly felt self-conscious. Drawing her hand up to the collar of her pyjama top, she flattened the green, silken fabric against her skin before turning to face him.

'It's been a while since I was last home,' Alexander said, neither looking nor speaking directly at her. Standing on the other side of the room, he was half-turned away from her, running his fingers over the spines of the books on her bookcase. 'Feels like longer,' he continued, pausing to look at her before turning back to the books.

Nodding, Mary moved to the bed and sat down. The lamp on the bedside table next to her cast the room in a sleepy glow. 'New Year's,' she said, still nodding, remembering the last time they had seen each other.

He hummed by way of reply and turned so that he was leaning against the bookcase.

'You haven't missed much,' she continued, her voice low and inexpressive. 'Not much has changed.' Alexander watched her as she spoke and she wondered why he was there. Beyond him, the curtains were drawn and the muted light of the room distorted the edges of his silhouette so that only the left side of his face was fully illuminated.

'I'm not so sure.' He was looking at the books again and spoke slowly. 'It seems to me as though some things have changed.'

His words — *the way he said them* — did something strange to her stomach and she couldn't help but move her right arm so that she was holding herself ever so slightly. He must have felt something too and so spoke again, his tone different this time.

'I rarely have time to read anything anymore.' He smiled at her and, with a thumb, indicated to her books. 'Well, aside from medical textbooks, of course.'

'Sounds delightful,' she replied, a smile, sharp and fleeting, curving the corners of her mouth.

Alexander let out a little laugh and nodded. 'Yeah. It certainly makes me want to try something else.'

'I can imagine.' Standing, Mary walked to the bookcase. Next to her, Alexander watched as her eyes moved over the shelves. Not stopping to look at him, she removed a book, flipped open the pages, then put it back. 'When I read,' she said, 'I have a rule—' she paused and, glimpsing him out of the corner of her eye, took a quick breath before continuing. 'One non-fiction, one fiction. It's something my father's always said. His method for avoiding being made a bore by all the economics he writes.'

Alexander laughed and so she did too. 'It's a good rule,' he nodded.

Eyes turned away, Mary gestured to the shelves. 'Would you like to borrow something?'

Another nod. A glance and she once again began looking at the books. Without saying anything, he waited, watching her fingers move over the covers. Crouching down, she reached for one of the books on the bottom shelf. Her pyjama top moved as she did, revealing a wonderful flash of skin where her hip curved into her waist.

'What are you in the mood for?' she asked as she selected another book from the bottom shelf. Alexander didn't reply and waited for her to stand up. She did, and placed three books, stacked on top of each other, on the shelf level with her hands before pushing them towards him. Quietly, he thanked her. She nodded, unblinking, the soft, orange light from the bedside lamp grazing the side of her face and the length of her neck.

'You look like a painting,' he whispered to her.

Eyes unmoved, each watching the other, he raised his hand then, reaching for her, slow and careful, stopping before he contacted the side of her neck, his fingers hovering above the place where her collar caressed her skin. She didn't recoil and so, eyes still on each other, he touched her. When he reached her collar unopposed, he grew bolder, and, slipping his hand under the fabric, gently pushed it away so as to expose her collar bone and part of her shoulder. The strange sensation in her stomach returned, Mary realised she was standing much too close to him. Lowering her voice to the same whisper he had used only a moment before, smoothing the syllables of her speech in an attempt to conceal her anxiety, she said, 'A good painting, I hope.'

Words, however, were fast becoming redundant. Alexander merely hummed in agreement, his fingers still on her skin. Her breathing had changed — it was quicker now — and he was so close to her that he could see the silent rising and falling of her chest. He traced his fingers back up her neck, not stopping until he reached her chin. Softly, he held her, cupping her face between his forefinger and thumb, before drawing her to him.

She didn't resist and allowed him to give it to her. Her first kiss. *Our first kiss.* It was all that she had dreamt it would be and, at the same time, entirely different. Tender, yet clumsy. Brash, yet somehow strangely beautiful. Softer than she could have ever imagined, even as the stubble that furred his cheeks bit the skin of hers.

Her eyes closed at their coming together and she wondered what she should do with her hands, whether she should touch him in return. As it was, he soon found a use for them, running his free hand over her shoulder and down her left arm to take her hand. Pushing their fingers together, the kiss was transformed into something firmer. Tenderness diffused into yearning and he was nudging her backwards with his body, guiding her towards the bed. Eager, and yet unsure, she let him lay her down on top of the quilt. She moved her eyes to the ceiling as he slid down her body to take off her trousers.

He must have liked what he found as he started kissing her there too. Flushed and flustered, she experienced it behind her eyelids. Flashes of colour brightened the darkness of her vision as he provoked in her feelings she had never experienced before. She dared not open her eyes for fear of seeing him — for fear that she wouldn't know what to do or what to say. Timeless moments slipped away and he returned to her, pushing his face into her neck, indulging in the scent of her hair, gently running the lobe of her ear through his teeth, making her wriggle and laugh, his hands everywhere.

Raising himself so that his face was over hers, he began to unfasten the buttons of her pyjama top. Eyes now open, she tilted her chin down to see him do it. A pause and his eyes returned to hers.

'Is this okay?' he asked in a whisper.

Hair pressed against the pillow, she nodded, and so he continued until there was nothing between them.

As obvious as his lust was, he was gentle with her. It was

painful, but pleasurable — more so than she had thought possible. He held her to him as he pushed his body into hers. A hand on the back of her head, fingers tangled in her curls, and his other on her thigh, holding her, thumbing her naked skin as he loved her.

*Love.*

That was not what it was. Mary knew that. But, it was okay. *One day it will be.*

Once he was in, it couldn't have been very long. Perhaps he could tell she was uncomfortable, perhaps he just couldn't hold back any longer. Pushing his face back against her neck, he buried himself there, mouth to her skin, kissing her, breathing her, his nose rubbing the soft, sweet spot behind her ear. And then, it was over. He was panting. She looked at him and saw that there was sweat on his forehead. Still over her, he lowered his face to hers and, softly, kissed her cheek before pulling out and rolling off her. On his back, staring at the ceiling, he rested his hand on her stomach and, seemingly absentmindedly, started to massage the soft skin around her belly button as he caught his breath. Lying next to him, she focused on the sound of his breathing and waited for him to say something.

He didn't, and as his breathing softened and the moment slipped into the past, her self-consciousness grew to the point that she needed to get up. Her voice barely above a whisper, she told him she needed to use the bathroom and, as delicately as she was able, slipped off the bed and hurried to the adjoining room.

As soon as she was through the door, she burst into tears. Holding herself, her other hand over her mouth to suppress the sobbing, she moved to the toilet and, lid closed, sat down. She wasn't sad. *That's not what these tears are.* She knew that variety all too well. No, these tears were something else. Tears of joy. In spite of it all, in spite of the circumstance, she was happy.

Emotions quietened, she stood and moved to the sink so as to wash her face. It was then that she noticed the blood on the lid of the toilet. Touching herself, she realised there was more. Some had trailed down her inner thigh and she immediately thought of the quilt on the bed and Alexander. As quickly as she was able, she cleaned herself and looked about the bathroom for something to wear. There was nothing and so, as naked as he had made her, she opened the door and stepped back into the bedroom.

He had put his boxer shorts back on but was still on the bed, sitting up with his back against the headboard. He turned to look at her when she re-entered the room and it was clear that he had been waiting for her. There was a strange expression on his face: his ever-soft brown eyes were scrunched at the corners, struggling somewhere between concern and surprise. There was no doubt that he had seen it. Mary moved to the bed and, anxious to cover herself, slipped under the bloodstained quilt. She felt him touch her shoulder.

'Are you alright?'

She nodded. 'Yes.'

A pause, and then, 'I'm sorry.'

She shuffled on the bedsheet and turned to look at him. 'Why?'

His cheeks were tinged red and she couldn't tell if it was

from physical exertion or embarrassment. He shrugged his shoulders and shook his head.

'You don't need to apologise,' she said. Both resting against the headboard, faces turned together, they held each other's gaze. Neither one turned away, and so, eyes full and free, they kept looking, each trying to discern the inner workings of the other's mind.

After a moment, his eyes relaxed and he nodded. 'Okay.'

Perhaps he felt obligated to stay, perhaps he stayed because he wanted to. She couldn't tell. Either way, he didn't immediately leave, as she thought he might. Slouching down the headboard, he joined her under the quilt so that he was leaning on his side, half-propped up by a pillow, his elbow against the mattress, his head resting on his hand. He didn't try to touch her again, but he spoke to her. About university. About the weather. About a piece of music he had heard playing on the radio. He didn't tell her anything special — to anyone else his words would have been mundane — but she was delighted to listen. She couldn't remember another time like it, and neither could he.

When his words were spent, he told her he was tired and that he should go back to his own bed. Careful not to pull the quilt off her as he got up, he dressed in silence before walking to the door. From the bed, she watched him leave, quiet, happy, confused, wondering what he would be like in the morning.

# Regnant

*It is the morning after Strawberry's Metamorphosed Yearning. Sophie is in the kitchen making breakfast.*

There was an art to it. Once the slice was separated from the loaf, she used a paring knife — *its edge plainer and blade sharper than the bread knife* — to define the shapes. A heart could be sculpted from a corner, a cloud carved from a rounded top, and a flower, *the most artful of all,* coaxed from a centre. Ten even incisions, two per petal, drawn into delicate pinched tips, *being certain to disregard slices with large air pockets beforehand.* A minute or two under the grill, turned midway, and the perfect brown was achieved. *That is once you're close to done with everything else, of course.*

To Sophie's mind, there was nothing worse than cold toast. A symptom of poor planning, and, culinarily, an indisputably awful experience, serving bread that was anything less than hot-enough-to-melt-butter-but-not-enough-so-as-to-melt-you was indefensible. Hard crusts discarded, cut and shaped ahead of time, she slipped the bread under the grill just as the egg whites changed colour. The sound of sizzling and she scooped a streak of fatty flesh from the pan. A second followed before, oven-gloved, she turned the toast. Cutlery already on the serving tray, she brought a coffee cup to it, retrieved the toast, buttered, baconed, milked the coffee, then arranged the eggs. Wobbling, fried and orange and ready to pop, they made the cheerful centres of her toasted flowers. The plate was warm and so she used a red gingham napkin to move it to the tray. A quick straightening of the edge, tucking the fabric under the knife and fork, and breakfast was ready.

Sophie held the tray steady as she climbed the stairs. First door on the right, it had been closed all morning. She shifted the tray of food into her right hand and tapped on the wood.

'My strawberry.'

She didn't know if he was still asleep and so kept her voice low.

'Breakfast's ready.'

More tray shuffling, coffee threatening to overspill, and she knocked on the door again. There was nothing. Sighing, Sophie remembered how miserable her son had looked when he said goodnight to her the evening before.

'It's just outside, dear.' She stooped to place the tray on the carpet. 'Don't let it get cold.'

At that, she stepped away and went to go back downstairs. As she did, however, a voice caught her attention. Turning, so that she was facing the door on the other side of the landing, Sophie brought her hand to her chest.

'Alex—'

The sound was interrupted by giggling. Soft and breathless, it was met by low, mumbling words. The two sounds melded to one and there was more laughter, more muffled than before. Standing outside Mary's bedroom door, Sophie raised her hand to her mouth. Twisting back to the other door, she scooped Alexander's breakfast from the carpet, steadied the tray, and slipped, silently, back downstairs to the kitchen. Abandoning the food on the table in the middle of the room, she closed the door and, back against it, arms wrapped around her middle, held herself.

*No.*

She squeezed herself.

*But, it would...*

Thoughts detaching from the known, she embraced the possible.

*He went to bed early last night.*

Sullen, brown eyes and a voice sad enough to sour milk. Mary had also excused herself. They had been watching one of their favourite films. It was unlike her to leave before the end.

*Then there was the quilt.*

Sophie very nearly squealed and had to move her hand to her mouth. A quick peek outside the door to confirm there was no one there in need of her and she hurried across the kitchen to the calendar which hung on one of the cupboards. A small amount of blood on the sheets was one thing — *women bleed* — but it was not the right time of the month — *our cycles are aligned* — and it should have certainly not been on the quilt — *unless she was sleeping on top of it.*

Mary and Alexander were sleeping together.

How could she have not noticed?

A creak from the other side of the kitchen and Sophie very nearly jumped out of her skin.

'Are you alright, my darling?'

Fumbling, flustered words and Sophie told her husband she was fine.

'The weather's most definitely changing,' Robert said as he walked into the kitchen. 'I'll be sad to say goodbye to summer.'

Sophie nodded and agreed.

'Is this for Alex?' Robert asked, gesturing to the, by now fast becoming cold, breakfast on the table.

Again, Sophie nodded.

'Do you want me to take it up to him? I'm going up—'

'No!' One long stride and Sophie moved to intercept her husband. Slipping her hands ahead of his, she pulled the tray away from him and, a sudden breath, pushed a smile onto her face. 'I—' facing her husband, she maintained her smile. 'I was thinking, contemplating, really, about how I probably shouldn't baby him any more.' Fingers still wrapped around the tray of food, she offered Robert an exaggerated shrug. 'He is a man now after all and—' She trailed off. Still looking at her husband, she made her smile wider. Robert, silent, nodded slowly.

*He cannot know.* Sophie unpeeled her fingers from the tray. *Not yet anyway.*

'Well,' it was Robert, 'I'm just going upstairs to get—'

'Don't go.' Sophie moved towards him. 'I'll get them for you. Eat some breakfast.' At that, she put her hand on her husband's arm and guided him to one of the chairs at the table. Pushing him into it, she picked up the plate of cold toast and placed it down in front of him.

*If he knows that he knows it will jeopardise everything. Worse still if—*

A sudden breath, an image of Robert Senior, grey and cackling, and Sophie shook her head.

She turned to her husband. 'Stay here and relax, my dear,' she said to him, her voice sweet and soft. 'You work so hard. Let me take care of you.' A kiss on his cheek and she gently cupped his face.

Robert smiled. 'Thank you, my darling.'

Sophie thumbed his face lovingly. 'I won't be a minute,' she smiled, then turned to leave the room.

She had to be careful on the stairs. *They might still be in there together and—*

'Good morning.'

The first door on the right opened and through it came Alexander. Fluffy hair and tired, heavy eyes, he was wearing the same shirt as the day before. The last step on the stairs, his mother kept her face subdued.

'Good morning, my strawberry.' She stepped around him so that her back was to Mary's door. 'Did you sleep well?'

Ruffling his hair with his hand, Alexander yawned and nodded.

'You seemed quite tired last night.'

Another nod from Alexander. 'Yeah,' he said, his voice all of a sudden darkening, the moroseness of the evening before inflating his every breath. 'I was.'

Slowly, Sophie nodded. 'Well,' she said, breathing deeply as she conjured a smile, 'I can make you some breakfast if you like.' Alexander nodded. 'Your father's in the kitchen. I'm just fetching him a fresh pair of socks. All that rain last night!' She gave a little laugh. 'I don't know how any of us managed to sleep!' She held his eyes, smiling, then, slipping away from the stairs and along the hallway, rushed into hers and Robert's bedroom.

*Be calm, Sophie.*

She hurried to the chest of drawers that housed her husband's underwear.

*If he knows that you know then—*

She opened the top drawer and pulled out a pair of black socks. Stitched into the sole in block blue letters was the day of the week Friday.

*Tammy only left on Tuesday.*

Sophie closed the drawer.

*Two nights.*

A squeeze of the socks.

*The blood on the quilt was yesterday.*

And so it had been a day.

*A single day.*

Still squeezing the socks, Sophie moved to the door.

*Surely that isn't long enough?*

But, it was meant to be. It had *always been* meant to be. And so it would be. *Regardless of the day of the week.*

Squashing the socks inside her hand, Sophie took a breath and left the room.

By the time she returned to the kitchen, Mary was up and out of bed also. Leaning against the worktop by the sink, hair coiled and chaotic, contained by a cream-coloured headband, she was waiting for the kettle on the stove. Alexander, along with his father, was sitting at the kitchen table.

'Good morning,' Sophie smiled as she entered the room.

Mary raised her head towards her and said good morning also.

'Did you sleep well?'

Mary nodded. 'Yes,' she said. 'Thank you.'

More smiling and nodding from Sophie and she handed her husband the socks.

'I didn't know you ate shapes.'

Robert looked up from his breakfast.

Across the table, Alexander nodded at the plate of food. 'Your toast,' he said, nodding his head again.

'Oh—' a smile and Robert, dabbing his mouth with the gingham napkin, took a quick sip of coffee. 'Oh, yes,' he continued, nodding at his son. 'Your mother did a lovely job.' He turned in his chair. 'Didn't you, my darling?'

Sophie was standing in front of the sink. More smiling. More nodding.

'You know, my strawberry,' a deep breath of air and Sophie stepped towards him, 'would it be alright if, just today, I made you some cereal instead?' She placed a hand on Alexander's shoulder and, smiling widely, squeezed him. 'Your sisters already ate, and so—' Her voice slipped away. Still smiling, Sophie turned and caught Robert's eye.

*If he knows that he knows.*

Alexander straightened in his chair. 'Yeah,' he said, slowly and then nodding. 'Sure. That's fine.'

Sophie smiled. 'Good. Thank you.' With that she released him and moved across the room. A bottle of milk from the fridge, a bowl from the oak sideboard by the door, and a box of cereal from the cupboard — reached on her tiptoes from the top shelf.

'There you are, my strawberry,' she said, setting the box down on the table next to him.

Alexander thanked her. Behind him, the water had finished boiling. Mary turned and lifted the kettle from the stove. The spice of cinnamon rushed the room as soon as the hot water hit the teabag.

'I'll take this upstairs,' Mary said after she had finished pouring her tea. 'I'll make myself something else in a bit.'

At the table, Robert smiled and nodded at her. Alexander simply ate his cereal in silence.

'Okay, my marshmallow,' Sophie said, watching her as she picked up her mug and moved to the door. 'Just let me know if you need anything.'

Mary stopped and, a strange, soft look, nodded at her.

*But, if she knows that I know...*

Eyes full and bright, Sophie smiled and nodded back. Behind her, spoon clinking and crunching, Alexander swallowed another mouthful of cereal.

After that, Robert struck up a conversation about a new biochemistry analyser he had seen advertised for sale. Fully automatic, with a robotic arm able to pipette reagents into sample tubes for analysis, it could manage many tests at a time. By contrast, his current, semi-automatic analyser only allowed for one test at a time, with each having to be set up individually. A fence also needed to be mended down the hill by the habitation buildings. Perhaps Alexander could look at it with him. The weather was worsening and, if left, the wear would only increase. In between cereal-spooning, Alexander nodded and said that he would. Sophie, meanwhile, stood by the sink, watching, but not listening, holding a cup of freshly brewed coffee to her lips.

***

It had been different for her. Wide smiles and effortless intentions, Robert had always been confident. When he had proposed to her, they had only been together a few months. *Three. To the day.* A series of love letters, punctuated by stomach-fluttering visits to each other's homesteads, and he had told her that he would always take care of her. She would be his, and — after he had finished his medical degree — he would be hers. Three months of courtship. Three years of engagement. It was a straightforward, sincere, assured agreement. *Robert has always known what he wants.* And, more importantly, he had never been afraid to allow himself to pursue such desires.

His son was not like that.

Sophie cracked the egg on the side of the bowl. Careful to pull the shell apart as cleanly as possible, she tipped the yolk into one half of the shell. A bowl below caught the white as it drained over the crack.

Softer than his father, apprehensive and principled, Alexander was self-punishing by nature. He was also incredibly stubborn. *That he does share with Robert.* Caged by rules of his own creation, he would martyr himself to prove a point. In this case — *which is, for Alex, the case of all cases* — Mary was the point. For many years, it seemed as though she was the hill upon which he had chosen to die. *The line he would never, under any circumstance, cross.* His grandpa's old red car. A begrudging acceptance whose fast freedom he had come to cherish. The same medical degree at the same university as his forebears. A convenient compromise that got him away from the pressures of home. Mary, the bride his father had selected for him from birth. An intrusion he could never allow. Sophie knew all too well why he had not returned home after New Year's.

Plug in the socket, she turned on the electric whisk and began to beat the egg whites.

It had been painful for her to watch her son torture himself. It had been even more painful to experience his withdrawal. If Mary was the hill, then they — she, his father, his grandfather, the very home in which they all lived together — were the path that drew him to her. He didn't want to walk it, had decided he couldn't walk it, and so had run off into the wilderness to beat himself a different one.

*Until now.*

Tammy's arrival had very almost broken Sophie's heart. Her departure had restored the fragmented parts. And yet, Mary's ascendence had done little to glue them back together. Too sudden, *too real*, it frightened her.

Thick, stiff peaks, the meringue was starting to form. Sophie added a tablespoon of sugar and continued to whisk the mixture.

*What does it mean? Why now?*

Would he promise to always take care of Mary, as Robert had promised her? Or, would it — after a series of secret meetings, sex, opportunities to blow off steam and somehow prove to himself that he didn't need the world that they had built for him — end in pain and disappointment?

Another spoonful of sugar into the bowl.

It had been different for her. But, Alexander wasn't his father. *And Mary isn't me.* And so, maybe there was hope. *Maybe she will be the one to tell* him *that he will always be taken care of.*

A final blitz of the whisk and the meringue was ready to be spooned into rough balls and baked in the oven. In just under an hour's time, they would be golden-brown, chewy-centred crusts of heaven. Sophie closed the door to the oven and, stepping to the sink, washed her hands.

Outside, the rain which had plagued the early morning had been driven away by the Sun. Regnant once more, long-limbed and golden, she stretched splendidly across the sky.

Mary was in the back garden. Long, slow, deep breaths, the grass soft under her bare feet, she was lazily supervising Guinevere and Aurélie as they pulled carrots from the plots in the vegetable garden. Hair drawn back off her face, she was standing, straight-backed and steady, with her left leg bent slightly at the knee and her right raised. Tucking her right foot behind the knee of her left leg, she, with a slow, careful extension of her arm, brought one of her hands over her head. Fists clenched, she pulled her other to her side. Long, slow, deep breathing and she held the stance.

Sophie carried a jug of juice down the steps which led from the back door. Placing it on the table which stood in the middle of the lawn, she watched Mary change stance. Expertly balanced, without returning her right leg to the ground, she turned her core so as to extend her foot out, toes sharp, into a kicking pose. She kept her eyes ahead and, as ever, her breathing long, slow, and deep.

When Mary had first fallen under Sophie's guardianship, she had attempted to encourage her to learn ballet. Her mother — so Sophie had known, but not understood — had already introduced Mary to *Taekwondo* and even — rather inappropriately, so Sophie thought, for a six-year-old girl — the

Japanese spear-wielding art of *Sōjutsu*. With their leg extensions and focus on balance and core strength, Sophie had thought such martial arts might segue into the much more suitable performance art of ballet, or, if Mary didn't enjoy that, gymnastics, or perhaps even figure-skating. As a girl Sophie had enjoyed horse riding. If needed, she could have always convinced Robert to buy a pony. But, Mary didn't want to do ballet. Neither was she interested in ice skates or animals or sewing or any of the other feminine pursuits Sophie had carefully exposed her to. Now, at almost twenty-one-years-old, Mary practised *Taekwondo* several times a week, possessed a third-degree black belt, and had recently started learning *Krav Maga* at the community hall in town.

'Would you like a drink, marshmallow?'

A long, slow, deep breath and Mary nodded her head. Bracelet chinking the side of the jug, Sophie poured the juice into a glass.

She was careful to make sure Guinevere and Aurélie stayed in the vegetable garden — carrying their drinks to them, rather than have them come over to her — so that she could speak with Mary alone. Seamless black leggings and a matching long-sleeve cropped top, Mary finished her stance and walked to the table. There was a small amount of perspiration on her brow from the Sun. She wiped it away with the back of her hand, then took a long drink of juice.

'Thank you, Sophie,' Mary said, nodding.

Sophie smiled in return. 'I was thinking, marshmallow,' she said as she watched the younger woman take another drink. 'Perhaps I could come with you next time.' Mary looked at her over the rim of her glass. 'The next time you go to one of your classes.'

A curious expression and Mary put her drink down on the table. 'One of my classes?'

Sophie nodded.

'*Taekwondo*?' Mary's lips stretched into a smile. '*Krav Maga*?'

'Whichever, dear.'

Mary picked up her glass again and took another sip.

'I thought,' Sophie continued, the tone of her voice sweet, 'that it might be good for you and I to spend more time together. You know,' she paused and made sure to meet Mary's eyes, 'just the two of us.'

A moment to assess her and, slowly, Mary nodded. 'I would like that,' she said. Then, a wide, giggling smile, 'But, it doesn't have to be *Krav Maga*.'

Giggling also, Sophie shook her head. 'No,' she said. 'I suppose not, dear.' Another giggle and she nodded, 'Thank you.'

Smiling, Mary nodded back at her.

'I—' Sophie looked away and, turning to the jug of juice, began fiddling with a glass, the one she had brought outside for herself, slowly pushing it around the table, her fingers on the rim. 'You do know, don't you, Mary—' a slow tilt of the head and she was again looking at the young, redheaded woman, 'that I'm here for you.' She paused and searched her eyes. 'If you need me. To talk or—' Another pause. 'Anything. Always.'

Her glass now empty in her hand, Mary slowly nodded. 'I do,' she said. 'Thank you.'

'Well,' a soft inhale of breath, 'I'm glad,' Sophie replied.

Mary returned her glass to the table. Gently, she placed her hand on Sophie's arm. 'Thank you,' she said again.

With that, there was something, *something small*, that passed between the two women. It was unseen, *but not unfelt*, and it told Sophie that Mary knew that she knew about her and Alexander, and that it was alright. *And, more than that, that* she *is alright.* A young woman who guarded her emotions as expertly as she guarded her core — defensive, arms pulled in, fists tight and clenched and ready to intercept offensive action — it was highly unlikely that she would open up to Sophie without good reason. *Tremendously good reason.* And so, Alexander's mother would have to content herself with the knowledge that Mary knew what she was doing — *knows what she wants* — and would, as such, be able to navigate the situation. It would not stop her worrying — *worrying about the both of them* — but it was a consolation of sorts.

'Have a think about what you'd like to do,' Mary said as she walked away from the table and back to the area of lawn on which she had been exercising. 'Something—' she quickly turned her head to look at Sophie, 'off the island.' A smile and she settled herself on the grass, bending over so that, feet and palms on the ground, her body was fully stretched. 'It would be nice to go somewhere just you and I.' Head upside-down, her curls, ever fighting to be free of their fastenings, tumbled over her face.

'I will, marshmallow,' Sophie nodded to her from the table. She collected the glasses together and picked them up along with the jug. 'Perhaps there's something crafty we could do together, a knitting project or—'

Her head still upside-down, Mary pulled a face.

'I've always wanted to try pot-making.'

'Really?'

'Ballet?'

A laugh. Arm stretching and Mary righted herself. Repositioning her feet, she looked across the grass at Sophie. Slowly, she smiled. 'I'll think about it,' she said.

Sophie matched her smile. Then, holding the jug to her chest, she started walking across the lawn and back to the house. When she reached the steps that led up to the back door, she stopped and, once more, turned to look at Mary.

'Oh, and marshmallow—'

One leg off the ground, Mary turned to look at her.

'The next time you exercise outside—'

Perfectly balanced, Mary nodded.

'You should do it on the front lawn,' Sophie continued. 'For, you know—' a smile, wide with mischief and knowing, pushed itself across her face. 'For the view.'

A sudden cough of laughter and Mary lost her balance. Sophie, porcelain-faced and smiling sweetly, simply giggled then went inside to check the meringues.

# Onus

*Set within the timeline of The Homestead's Act I, some time after the events of Chapter Ten but before the farewell of Chapter Fourteen, it is, in many ways, an ordinary day in the Wheatleigh house. And yet, out of sight of his parents, Alexander is being consumed by crisis. Mary represents both the source and the solution.*

He had disappeared again. Spent coffee grounds and breadcrumbs in the sink, he wouldn't be back until dinner time.

'Did he tell you where he was going?'

Leaning against the oak sideboard by the door, Mary had her nose in a newspaper. 'No,' she said without raising her eyes from the page. *Nine across, 'burden of responsibility'.*

'He seemed—' a slow pause from the other side of the kitchen, 'better, last night, don't you think?'

Pencil in her hand, Mary hovered over the paper. *Four letters, third letter 'u'.* 'No,' she murmured. 'No, I don't think so.'

Standing in front of the table close to the range cooker, Sophie simply sighed. A moment to readjust the sleeves of her blouse, pushing them up her arms and into the crooks of her elbows, and she returned to the lump of dough that she was kneading.

As it was, Mary knew precisely where Alexander was, not because he had told her, but because it was where he always went. Pebbles in the wheel arches of his car, he drove along the beach, out of sight of the house, turning off just before the causeway so as to make it seem like he had left the island.

He had been quieter than usual the previous evening. Aside from the mandatory pleases and thank yous — *sallow features and salad bowl pleasantries* — barely a word was heard from him all dinner. Everyone had noticed, but had tried to ignore it all the same. Finger-fidgeting from Sophie and wary, sideways glances when he thought no one else was looking from Robert. Mary had held her breath. Sat opposite him, she had waited for him to nudge her, *socked-feet under the table*, but he hadn't. He had merely finished his food and left. Then, later, when they were both in their bedrooms, he had come to her.

Unlike the times before, he had simply wanted to talk. Fluffing his hair with his hand, the cord of his dressing gown loose about his waist, he had stood over by the window, contemplating, deeply, about how and why they were where they were — and how it might be if it were otherwise. The world was such a vast place; it made no sense that they could change it. And, even if they could, nothing ever stayed the same forever. Lethargic, the syllables of his speech soft and slurring, he was unapologetically stoned.

Turning from the window to look at her, he had then asked her if she wanted to go swimming. Cross-legged on the bed, she had reminded him that it was the middle of the night. And so, he had joined her under the covers and, his words muffling into the pillow, had explained to her the philosophies of Absurdism and the fundamental meaninglessness of the universe. *Purpose is a human construct, with silence being the only certainty*. Soon after that, he had fallen asleep.

'Would you mind checking on the girls, marshmallow?' A final, long, elastic stretch and Sophie lifted the dough into a floured banneton. 'I'll be finished here soon.'

Mary nodded and started folding the newspaper. 'Mathematics?' she asked.

'Yes,' Sophie confirmed. A soft smile and she added, 'Guinny will probably be pouting for the piano. Providing she's done most of the work, tell her she can play.'

Mary said that she would. Leaving the newspaper on the sideboard, she left the kitchen and crossed the hallway to the sitting room.

There were teddy bears and crayons scattered on the rug and, in the middle of them, was Aurélie, happily drawing the hands on printed clock faces. Purple for the hour hand, and pink for the minute, she and her bears were fast mastering how to tell the time. Beyond, the door to the study was ajar, and sitting behind the desk was Guinevere, pouting, as her mother had supposed she would be.

'Can I finish now?' she asked as soon as she saw Mary crouch to inspect her little sister's clock-face drawings. 'It's pointless, you know.'

Mary glanced up from the rug and grinned at her. *The philosophies of Absurdism*. 'How much have you done?' she asked Alexander's sister.

'All of them. Well, more than half.' Sucking the end of her pencil, Guinevere pushed a piece of paper across the desk.

Mary caressed Aurélie's head, stood, and moved to the

office. 'That doesn't look like more than half,' she remarked as she examined the worksheet. Then, eyes raised and a quick quirk of her lips, she added, 'Perhaps you need to revisit fractions.'

More pencil sucking and Guinevere thrust out her lower lip.

A smirk and Mary folded her arms across her chest. 'Thirty-nine over sixty-five in its simplest form?'

'Three-fifths.'

'156 over...' smiling, Mary elongated the syllables as she spoke, '228.'

A moment to calculate. 'Thirteen over nineteen.'

'Tell me what complementary angles are.'

'Angles that add up to ninety degrees.'

'An irrational number?'

'An infinite decimal with no repeating set of consecutive digits.'

'Two, three, five and *x* have an average equal to four. What is *x*?'

'Six.'

'And,' another elongated syllable and Mary laughed, 'how long is a piece of string?'

At that, Guinevere huffed and spat out the pencil. Still laughing, Mary slid the worksheet back across the desk. 'Sophie said you have to do most of it. Don't shoot the messenger.'

Even so, Guinevere stuck her tongue out at her. Grinning, Mary returned the gesture before leaving her to finish her work.

Back in the kitchen, Sophie was sweeping away the last

remnants of dough from the table after having returned the jar of flour to the pantry. The dough, which would metamorphose to a loaf before the day was out, was on top of the stove, covered by a tea towel as it soaked in the ambient heat of the cooker.

'Do you need help with anything else?' Mary asked as she collected her newspaper from the sideboard.

A smile as she washed her hands at the sink and Sophie shook her head. 'No, my marshmallow.' Another smile. 'Thank you.'

Mary nodded and, tucking the paper under her arm, returned to the hallway. Crossword unfinished, she left it on the coffee table in the sitting room before pulling on her boots and leaving through the front door.

It was cool outside. The Sun was shining and yet seemed to make little difference; cold, but not unpleasant. Still, Mary wound her scarf around her neck as she crossed the gravel driveway towards the hill which slipped down to the causeway. The oak trees were shedding their leaves above and the ground was a watercolour symphony of reds and oranges. On the side of the road, lichen-covered boulders pushed out from the soil, brethren of the trees with roots too, alive in their own way, rolling into smaller rocks and soft-edged pebbles and eventually the sea. Slipping her hand into a weathered nook, Mary pulled herself over one of them and dropped down onto the other side. At the end of the road, the sea was in. His little red car trapped on the beach by a wall of water, she would have to go the difficult way if she wanted to be with him.

The car was full of smoke. Inside, a black hole of expectation and indecision, he was collapsing into himself.

'Have you gone for a swim yet?' Mary asked as she opened the passenger door.

Slouched in the driver's seat, Alexander was staring at the sea. 'It's not safe out there,' he mumbled, then, brown eyes wide, turned to look at her as she climbed into the car to sit next to him. 'Close the door,' he instructed, unsmiling and in a sudden whisper.

Narrowed eyes and a quizzical smile, she did as he told her, coughing, quickly wafting some of the smoke away from her face. 'How can you breathe—'

He interrupted her with a shush.

'Alex—'

He shushed her again, this time moving his hand to cover her mouth. 'Don't,' he whispered. 'They'll hear us.'

Underneath his fingers, Mary laughed. 'Who?'

Eyes returning to the sea and across the windscreen to the side window and along the beach and, shoulder-twisting, round to the back window, he replied, 'Did they follow you?'

'No,' she said through his fingers. 'They think you've gone into town.'

Alexander shook his head. 'No, no, no. Not them.' Still holding her, he once again looked outside the car. 'I mean *them.*' A gulp. 'The others.'

Mary strained in her seat to look around him and out of his window. His eyes were fixed on the beach, and yet there was no one there. Sitting back, she first shook her head, then licked his fingers, forcing him to remove his hand from her mouth. 'Who are the others?' she asked.

Whispering, the tension in his facial features visible as he did, he simply said, 'The sub-homos.'

At that, Mary started laughing. Alexander, however, was less than amused. His fingers back over her mouth, he shook his head and — big, brown eyes frozen — pleaded with her to stop.

'They're going to eat me, Mare,' he trembled. 'You too. Both of us when they find us.'

From where he sat, in the haze of the cannabis he had been smoking, everything he said not only made sense, but was distinctly terrifying. Mary, meanwhile, could only laugh.

'Alex,' she giggled, muffled underneath his fingers. 'That's ridiculous.'

'No, no,' he said, furiously whispering, shaking his head, 'it makes so much sense.'

'No—' Mary laughed and once again shook his fingers from her mouth. 'No,' she repeated. 'It really doesn't. Think about it—' she extended her hands out in front of her and gestured to the windscreen of the car. 'Do you see any sub-homos?'

Eyes darting, he shook his head.

'So,' she said, 'why are you worrying about them?'

Observable concentration and he seemed perplexed by the question. Mary started laughing again. Outside the car, a wave crashed into nearby rocks, sending spray up onto the windscreen. Runaway laughter, another wave, then Mary shook her head. 'Christ, Alex—' she reached for the door handle. 'I can hardly breathe in here. I'm getting light-headed.' Opening the door, she started coughing and climbed out of the car. Yet another wave on the rocks. This time, the spray hit her face.

'Are you sure you've parked far enough back?' she called to

him above the sound of the raging tide. Under her feet, the ground was wet. Hands on either side of the steering wheel, Alexander simply shook his head and started laughing.

And so, they left the car on the pebbles, clambering over the rocks to higher ground as the sea salted its tyres.

'Feeling better?' Mary asked him once they were settled against the wind-weathered remnants of a tree.

Alexander relaxed his head against the old trunk and shrugged. An almost smile tugged the corner of his lips. Mary grinned and leant back so that her head was next to his. Ahead of them, the sea was wild and grey. Huddled against the tree, cheek-to-cheek and wind-whipped on the crest above the beach, all they could see was water and red curls.

'Guinevere was trying to get out of algebra earlier,' Mary said after a moment of quiet.

'I don't blame her,' Alexander said. 'It's pointless.'

Mary laughed and a gust of wind rushed over the hill, forcing her to push her hands into the pockets of her jacket. Next to her, she could feel Alexander shuffle against her arm. Another moment of quiet passed before she spoke again.

'Do you ever think about what it was like?' she asked, slowly and in a low voice. 'When we were like that.'

Below them, the sea was lapping at the front tyres of Alexander's car.

*Like that.* She meant when they were children. *When we were not like this.*

'Not really,' he said. Another gust of wind, stronger than the last. It was getting colder.

A small murmur of agreement and he felt Mary's curls

brush against his cheek as she nodded. He took a deep breath and looked out at the sea.

'I—' she retreated. Silence, and she tried again, 'I don't think you should do this again.'

They turned so that they were facing each other. Their noses very almost touching, they were eye-to-eye.

'The cannabis,' Mary whispered to him. 'I think you should stop.'

Looking at her looking at him, he could see that it hurt her to love him.

'You—' she stopped again and, so close, he could taste the sweetness of her breath. 'I just don't think you need it.'

*Because I have her.*

Alexander pressed a smile onto his face. 'Okay,' he said slowly. An unsteady half smile and he dropped her eyes and turned to the ground. Then, through the fabric of his jumper, he felt her hand slip out from the pocket of her jacket. Without saying anything, it found his. Awkward fingers squashed between their two bodies, it was a clumsy, childish union.

He didn't pull away.

He wanted to say something, thought that perhaps he ought to say something, but he couldn't, and so he didn't. Instead, quiet, cheek-to-cheek on the wind-whipped crest above the pebble beach, they watched the waves together, waiting for the tide to retreat, one lost at sea, the other willing him to return to shore.

# Ruby

*After leaving the island at the end of The Homestead's Act I, Mary has been living with her father for several weeks. A hundred miles away, Alexander continues his university studies — alone and increasingly frustrated after Mary cuts communications with him. He will have to wait until Strawberry's Gingerbread Spice, and more properly The Homestead's Chapter Twenty, for peace to be restored.*

She was punishing him to prove that she could.

He had sent his most recent message late last night, only a few minutes before midnight. Short and pleading, she had already been asleep — mobile phone switched off on her bedside table. When she discovered it the next morning, her hand slipping, sleepily, out from under the covers so as to draw her phone to her, she read it twice, smiling as she did, before returning her phone to the table. By the time she was dressed, he would have sent another, *and perhaps even another.* They would be similarly supplicating, inciting melodrama by making use of words like 'mercy' and 'torture'. *M, have mercy, you know that's not what I meant. Six days is torture.* Today would make it seven. *And so maybe there will be two by the time I'm finished dressing.*

At first she had found the silence difficult. She had been upset, of course — *you can just catch the train back afterwards* — but messages from him had very quickly grown into every crack and crevice of her daily life, providing her with a structure she had come to depend upon, and dared not see disappear. Because of that, buckling their communications had been less than ideal. She missed their long phone conversations. The sound of his voice. The sight of his face whenever they video called. Happily, he was still sending emails and text messages for her to read. *And read them I do.* After all, each time she did, he would see that she had — *which is the most excruciating part of the punishment.*

Slipping out of her pale, pink pyjama bottoms, Mary reached for a fresh pair of underwear from her top drawer. Behind her, on her bedside table, her phone buzzed. A smile, followed by a moment to pull up her pants, and she moved to check the message.

*Good morning.*

He was typing and so, crossing her bedroom back to her chest of drawers, she left him to it.

It had started as teasing. Sexual theatrics that were fun to begin with, but all too soon exposed an upsetting well of mismatched intentions and inconsideration. *Come over so I can play with you. Just for the night. I've got a long day tomorrow — you should be there when I'm done.* There was nothing else behind it. He wouldn't admit to missing her. Wouldn't say he wanted her there for any reason other than sexual gratification. Told her that she could *just catch the fucking train back afterwards.* In the end, it had been necessary to pull away.

Tights and skirt, and Mary looked at her phone again.

*Did you sleep well?*

A smile and she turned the screen off. He would tell her about any dreams he had had next. University stuff. Going home. *Being chased by a giant bird with old man's voice.* Tucking her top into the waistband of her skirt, Mary laughed. Like most nights, she had dreamt of him. They had both been children, exploring rock pools together. It was the sort of thing that — even if she hadn't been ignoring him — she knew better than to share with him.

*I had a nice dream last night.*

Moving the phone to her dressing table, she left the screen on, propping it against her mirror so that she could see what he sent as she did her hair.

*You were in it.*

A small smile and she waited to see what he would say next. There was no icon to indicate that he was typing. Slowly, sitting in front of the mirror, she started to loosen the headband she wore at night to keep her curls in place.

'What happened in it?' she asked aloud, eyes still on the screen of her phone.

Still no typing. There was, it seemed, no more to tell. Looking away, Mary returned to her headband, freeing her curls and hydrating them with the hair oil she kept on her dressing table.

Her father was already downstairs.

'Good morning, Daddy.'

Piles of paper spread across the kitchen table, he looked up at her and smiled. 'Good morning, my love. Sleep well?'

Mary nodded and moved to the fridge to start preparing

breakfast. 'Have you eaten?' she asked, turning to glance at him.

Ern shook his head. 'Not yet,' he said.

Smiling, Mary nodded. 'I'll make you something.'

He thanked her after that. Tucking her phone into her cardigan pocket, Mary reached into the fridge for the eggs and butter before carrying them across the kitchen to the stove.

'What are your plans for the day?'

Mary cracked an egg against the side of a bowl. 'I haven't decided yet,' she said. Returning the empty shell to the tray, she reached for another egg.

Her father nodded, removing his glasses from his nose. 'I have a couple of lectures later this morning.' Handkerchief in his other hand, he started to polish the lenses. 'The interdependence of oligopolistic markets,' he continued, pausing, momentarily, to look across the kitchen at his daughter.

Standing at the worktop, her back was to him. 'Kinked demand curve theory?'

Her father, clearing his throat, nodded. 'Yes.' Another throat clear and he returned his glasses to his face. 'Then into resource depletion and whatnot.'

Moving to wash her hands under the tap, Mary turned and caught her father's eye. 'Perhaps another time,' she said, smiling.

At the table, Ern matched her smile. 'Alright, my love.' A nod and he watched her move back to the eggs. A fork into the bowl and she started to beat them together. 'So long as you know I'm always happy to have you there.'

Pausing, Mary turned to look at her father. 'I know, Daddy,' she said. Then, smiling, she added, 'Thank you.' Another nod from Ern and she returned to making their breakfast.

As it was, Mary had been in and out of her father's university lectures since she was little. A widower wed to his work, it had often been easier for Ern to bring his daughter along with him — sitting her at the back of the room, quietly, with a book in hand — than to arrange for her to be looked after by someone else. It had been a less than conventional childhood, one which, years and many economics lectures later, had resulted in Mary being more than familiar with price rigidity within an oligopoly.

The kitchen was quiet now, the only sounds being those of paper shuffling across the table and eggs scrambling in the frying pan. Then, just as their toast finished in the toaster, a buzzing sound came from Mary's pocket. Leaving the eggs and the toast for a moment, she pulled out her phone and opened the message.

*What are you eating?*

A smile and she slipped her phone back into her pocket.

Her father had tidied his work from the table. Helping her set the knives and forks, he took the plates from her after that, placing them on the table in front of their respective seats. Two mugs of tea were brewing on the worktop. A splash of milk in both and Mary joined her father at the kitchen table.

'Thank you, my love,' Ern said as he scraped a mound of scrambled eggs onto the piece of toast he had just cut.

Across the table, Mary, already chewing, simply nodded.

Another mound of scrambled eggs and Mary's phone vibrated in her pocket. Pausing to take a sip of tea, she reached to retrieve it. Placing it on the table, she swiped the screen to unlock it and open the message. *Eggs?* Hand to her mouth, Mary resisted a grin.

'You know,' Ern said, 'I was considering keeping this rotation next year.'

Across the table, Mary looked from her phone to her father.

'Starting with oligopolies,' he continued, 'and then working my way to monopolies.'

On the phone, the typing icon appeared on the screen. Mary again glanced between it and her father. 'I think that's a good idea,' she said, raising her eyes so as to smile at Ern.

'Quite,' he said, nodding as he cut into his toast. 'It's useful — especially in the run up to Christmas — for the students to see non-price competition for market share in action. Christmas advertisements. Pressing brand loyalty and such.'

Still smiling, Mary once more agreed with her father. Another vibration from her phone and she, eyes darting, looked down at the screen.

*Black tea or something fancy?*

Fast typing, then another vibration.

*And by fancy, I mean weird and awful-smelling.*

Eyes on the message, Mary started laughing. On the other side of the table, her father was grinning.

'What's that, my love?' A small sip from his mug and Ern watched as his daughter raised her eyes to meet his.

'Oh,' Mary, a smile on her face, shook her head, 'it's nothing.'

Ern put his mug down on the table. 'It doesn't sound like nothing,' he said, chuckling. 'Are you watching one of those funny videos?' He made a swirling motion with his finger. 'I saw one, well, one of my students, actually, showed me one with a cat that—'

On the table, Mary's phone vibrated yet again.

*Your father's there, isn't he?*

An even wider smile pushed itself across Mary's face. More laughter and she shook her head. 'I'm sorry, Daddy,' she apologised, looking across at Ern, fumbling to turn the screen of her phone off. She swiped it from and under the table so as to stuff it back into her cardigan pocket. 'It's nothing,' she said again after the phone was gone.

Across from her, Ern had his eyes on her. A smile and he, knife and fork in hand, returned to his breakfast. More toast cutting. Under the table, Mary's phone continued to vibrate.

'I'll put it on silent,' Mary mumbled, hurriedly moving it, once more, between the table and her pocket so as to adjust the settings.

*Am I disturbing you?*

Buzzing.

*Say and I'll stop.*

More buzzing.

*One word.*

Tapping the screen, Mary put her phone into silent mode. When she was done, her father appeared to be waiting for her. 'Is everything alright?' he asked.

Nodding, Mary said that it was.

'It's only—' pausing, and Ern put his knife and fork down on his plate. 'You've been quite preoccupied recently.' He was gesturing towards her, finger swirling. 'With your phone and—'

Mary gave him a smile. 'It's nothing, Daddy.' She held his eyes for a second, then attempted to return to her breakfast.

'You know,' Ern continued, his voice slower and lower than before, 'you can tell me anything, my love.' His face was soft. Looking across the table at him again, Mary, mirroring his softness, nodded.

'I know,' she said. A pause and then, 'But it really is nothing. It's just Alex.'

Opposite, her father looked confused. 'Alex?'

Mary nodded.

Sustained confoundment and then, shrugging it away, Ern's expression flickered to a smile, before changing again to creases of concern. 'Is he well? Robert? Sophie?'

Mary moved forward in her chair a little. 'Yes,' she said, looking at him, 'They're fine, Daddy.' A small smile and she nodded at her father. 'I spoke on the phone with Sophie only yesterday.' Another nod and Ern's expression lightened. Mary reached for her tea. 'Alex is at university and—' She was fiddling with the mug handle. Stopping, she again looked across at her father. Smiling, from both, and there was a moment of quiet.

Ern was the next to speak. 'Of course,' he said, nodding animatedly as he looked at her. Even more nodding and he made his smile wider. They returned to quiet after that. Mary picked up her cutlery and cut off a piece of toast. Under the table, her phone, although now muted, was probably still receiving messages.

*A duopoly.*

She chewed on the egg and toast.

*They'll end up fighting for market share in an attempt to establish a monopoly.*

Glancing up from her breakfast, Mary smiled across the table at her father. Eating his own, he, slowly, smiled back at her.

*And so there'll be competition by Christmas.*

Reaching for her mug, she brought it to her mouth and, her father's slow, uncertain smile unchanged the entire time, quietly finished her tea.

***

There was a new shop on the corner of Market Street. Men's apparel, specialising in formal attire, grooming, *and a comprehensive outerwear edit*, the building had previously housed an antique shop that, for one reason or another, had barely opened its doors in years. Now thoroughly remodelled, with polished hardwood floors, soft lighting, and elegant lines of jackets hung from brass clothes rails, the shop sought to attract a specific clientele — the gentleman shopper, academically-affiliated, with money to spare.

'Would you like it gift wrapped?' the assistant asked as he scanned the small, square box at the till. Standing opposite, her purse in hand, Mary nodded and thanked him. A reciprocal nod and the assistant reached for the mound of tissue paper on the shelf behind him. Careful, expert folds and the box was wrapped. A blue and yellow paisley pocket square made of the softest rolled silk, it would remain that way until Christmas morning.

'And these?' the assistant continued, nodding at the other items Mary had brought to the front of the shop.

'No,' she said. 'Leave those.'

A nod and he picked up the socks, scanning them into the till. They were dark red and green argyle-patterned. On the counter beside them there was a second blue and grey pair. The assistant scanned them too, before placing both pairs inside a shopping bag. She would give them to her father when she got home.

Mary hadn't heard from Alexander for several hours. She had read his last message, hurrying up the stairs after breakfast, in the doorway between her bedroom and the landing. *I have a DOS meeting in half an hour.* His words had been followed by an upside-down smiley face. Frustrated resignation, he had told her that his Director of Studies had been trying to convince him to change his third year specialist study choice from psychology to genetics since he had made the decision back in March. Only a couple of weeks before the end of term, he would no doubt push hard at the meeting — the window for Alexander to make the modification fast closing.

'Hello! I did wonder if I would see you today!'

Mary gave a small smile and entered the shop. Over her head, the bell on the door jingled as she stepped towards the counter.

'Is it ready?' she asked, shuffling her handbag from her shoulder so as to set it down on the wooden surface.

Opposite, the shopkeeper, an uncomfortable man who had operated a bespoke leather shop inside the city's old covered market for the last couple of decades, was encouraging the young woman to lean in closer.

'It is,' he nodded, smiling. 'But—' a raised finger and his smile grew. Silent, and with her back straight, Mary waited for him to continue. A sudden burst of unrestrained, chortling laughter and the man touched her on the arm. 'You have to take a look at some of my new merchandise first!' Stepping out from behind the counter, the man continued to encourage the young woman towards him. 'Patent leather,' he announced, gesturing to a pair of deep brown men's shoes. The leather was glossy and caught in the light of the shop as he lifted them from the stand on which they stood. 'I only finished them last week,' the man announced, pushing the shoes towards Mary.

Eyes moving slowly between the man and his shoes, she didn't say anything.

'I thought your father might like a new pair,' shoe man continued, shaking the shoes a little. 'I can—' fingers running the laces, he moved down to caress the toe cap, 'add a little something-something. Stitching. Broguing. Perforations wouldn't take me very long,' he raised his eyes to look at Mary. 'Plus, they're his size.'

'I'll think about it,' she replied, tone expressionless. The man, standing too close to her, nodded and returned the shoes to their stand. Mary took a step back. 'So, Geoffrey,' she said, 'can I see it?'

At that, the shopkeeper, Geoffrey, led her back towards the counter. 'Just a moment,' he said, moving from her. 'It's in the back.' A gesture and he left her beside the till, the door leading to the back thumping against its frame as he disappeared.

The shop was overflowing. Wallets and folios. Satchels and

ladies' handbags. Hanging from a rack behind the counter, arranged by length and colour, was a series of leather belts. Each boasted an elegantly-engraved metal buckle. Shoes, however, were the shopkeeper's specialism. Hand-crafted artistry borne from years of experience, the man's abundant enthusiasm for his trade was famous, the result being that, over the years, several pairs of boots — both wanted and unwanted — had made their way from his shop into Mary's wardrobe.

Geoffrey was still in the back. Waiting for him, Mary heard a vibration come from inside her handbag.

*I would appreciate a message from you.*

A slow, twisting smile and, turning the screen off, she returned her phone to her bag.

'Here it is!' Looking up, Mary saw the shopkeeper come back through the door. 'The brass has polished up nicely.' Moving to stand next to her, he pushed an old, elaborately-carved wooden box across the counter towards her. Mary took it from him and lifted the lid.

Inside the box was a compass. Made of brass, antique, with gorgeous engravings on its face which laid out the cardinal directions, it was both a purposeful and beautiful device. Older than she knew, and of special significance, it had been crafted to provide stabilisation in stormy seas. Mary tilted the compass back and forth on her hand. At its centre, a small red stone — *a ruby* — caught in the light. She turned the compass over and inspected the reverse.

'You've done a good job,' she said, eyes moving from the navigational device to Geoffrey. A thumb over the compass' cool, metal back, she felt the curves of Alexander's initials.

'I'm glad you like it,' Geoffrey said, nodding as he watched her examine his engraving.

Mary nodded. 'It's what I wanted.'

'Where did you say you got it from again?' Geoffrey asked, eyes shifting from the compass to the young woman.

A fleeting, half-smile from Mary. 'I didn't.' With that, she returned the compass to its box. The distinctive smell of brass saturated the air between them, then she closed the lid. A moment to secure it inside her handbag, and, shifting the bag to her shoulder, she indicated that she would like to pay.

'Remember the shoes,' Geoffrey said to her as he watched her put her purse away. 'Let your father know.'

Mary nodded and said that she would.

'I'll see you again soon, then,' the shopkeeper continued as she walked to the door. Shuffling her bag as she did, she reached for the handle. A ring of the bell, a final goodbye, and she was gone.

***

*You're being unreasonable, M.*

'No, Alexander, you are.'

The typing icon.

*A week is long enough. I don't know what you want me to do.*

'Offering an apology would be a good place to start.'

She was stretched out on her bed. Still dressed, mobile phone in one hand, compass in the other, she was also wearing the jacket he had given to her the last time they had been together.

*I'm sorry.*

A short laugh. 'One that you actually mean!'

Silence, and then, appearing, pausing, then there again, the typing icon.

*Immature.*

'Imbecile!' Longer laughter this time and, closing her fingers around the compass, she rolled over onto her stomach.

It was evening and Mary had not long finished eating with her father, he, as was his custom, having returned home late after a long day at work. They had eaten the aubergine *parmigiana* that she had made with the vegetables she had bought from the market earlier in the day. Rooting around in the back of the freezer whilst waiting for him, she had found a tray of chops and, after determining that they were probably still safe to eat, had cooked them also. Over aubergine, meat and wine, her father had told her about a society meeting he had planned for the end of term, then thanked her for his new socks. Smiling as she listened to him, she had made sure that her phone was upstairs, muted, on her bedside table.

Now, he was typing again. No doubt also in his room, likewise lying on his bed, she could taste his torture.

*You can't keep this up forever.*

Mary smiled and watched as another message appeared.

*A day more.*

More typing.

*Then you'll crack.*

Giggling and she placed the phone down on the bed.

As it was, Mary had no intention of keeping it up forever. In two weeks' time, he would return home from university for Christmas. She would be there, and then — *and only then* — would she speak to him again.

*Please don't keep this up.*

A wider smile and she glanced at the compass, its needle swaying around the ruby.

He went quiet after that. The typing icon disappeared, but she knew he was still there, perhaps waiting, so she imagined, in agonised silence, stubbornly expecting her to break the stalemate and send him something. Leaving her phone on the bed, she, still lying on her stomach, tugged on the sleeves of his jacket so that they reached all the way to her knuckles, then held the compass in both hands.

She had first seen the compass a very long time ago. Forgotten at the bottom of — *of all things* — a large wooden box that resembled a pirate captain's chest, they had used it to locate rubies. *That's why there's one on the needle.* An ancient treasure finder, the compass had, so they whispered to each other, been stolen from the pirate captain by Alexander's grandfather after he had caught him searching for loot on the island. The old man hadn't understood the object's magic, and so had resigned it to the chest. *We did though.* Smiling as she looked again at the ruby, Mary remembered how they had found their first treasure. An ethereal figment, *the sort that only children are able to see*, it had been high up in a tree, shining red in the midday Sun, calling for them to climb up and claim it. Compass tucked into one of his back pockets, he had dangled from the branch, legs looped around it, hair fluffy over his eyes as he held his hands down so as to pull her up. The compass had slipped out, falling to the ground, but he had not once let go of her, and promised that he never would. When she had seen it again, helping the old man to search for something in the clutter-heavy crawl space which occupied the eaves of his cottage, she knew she had to reclaim it. There were, after all, still rubies to be found, and she knew it would help Alexander to realise not only where he had been, but where he was, and, *most importantly*, that wherever he would end up was entirely his decision. The compass, and everything that it represented, was his — *and always has been.*

Leaving both the compass and her phone on the bed, Mary shuffled out of Alexander's jacket and slowly got changed into her pyjamas. By the time she was finished, there was a message waiting for her. Tapping the notification, she realised he had sent her a voice message. Stomach-fluttering, and, sitting down on the bed, she murmured, 'That's different.' Reaching again for the compass, she tapped the play button.

'Mary,' his voice was soft — *whispering* — and she could hear his breathiness against the microphone. 'I wish you were here with me.' He sighed after that. Mary, still holding the compass, lay back on the bed waiting for the message to continue. 'I really do. If only—' a pause and there was the beginning of a laugh. 'If only,' he continued, 'to tell you how ridiculous you're being!' He was laughing properly now, loud, full sounds into the microphone of his phone. Listening to him on the bed, Mary also started laughing.

'You really are!' he carried on, laughter saturating every syllable. 'So ridiculous! It's been a week, Mare!'

Clutching the compass to her chest, Mary was giggling.

'Is this punishment?' Alexander continued in the message. 'Because it's working!' More laughter and he, breathless, chuckled, 'I probably shouldn't have told you that.'

Laughing with him, Mary shook her head. 'No,' she giggled. 'You shouldn't have.'

Through the phone, the laughter slowly faded. Eventually, Alexander sighed. ‘I had that meeting today,’ he said. ‘Also, ridiculous.’ His voice was low, the lightness of a moment ago gone. ‘He brought up changing again. To genetics. Predictable, right?’

Listening, she nodded.

‘I don’t know why they’re all so—’ he paused, searching, ‘colluding.’ His voice became softer then. ‘Do you think my father asked him? Goff, that is. To pressure me to change?’

Quiet on the bed, Mary absorbed his words. She could still hear his breath on the microphone. ‘I don’t know, Alex,’ she whispered. Her curls were soft against her pillow as she shook her head. ‘I don’t know.’

‘Me neither,’ the recording continued. He gave another sigh after that, and she could hear him moving, his bed creaking as he readjusted himself. ‘I—’ he paused, seemingly thinking. ‘I just want to be free to make my own choices.’

‘I know you do.’ She was still whispering.

‘He said—’ he stopped, this time not to sigh, but to contain a chuckle, ‘he said, “it’s in your genes—”’ a breath of sniggering laughter, ‘No, really, Mare, I didn’t make that up, he said that—’ More laughter, more chaotic, with Mary mirroring him, clutching her chest as she giggled on the bed. ‘Ridiculous, right?’

She nodded. ‘That is ridiculous.’

‘So,’ he continued, ‘that’s why I thought about my father—’ the laughter was growing again, ‘whether he’d sent Goff a transcript or something, wince-worthy humour included.’

Holding onto the compass, Mary closed her eyes as she

giggled. Next to her on the bed, Alexander was laughing with her.

'Anyway,' Alexander said, chuckling still, 'I should let you go. Clearly, I'm pestering you.'

A grin pushed itself across Mary's face.

'Goodnight, Mary.' A final breath and the recording ended.

Mary reached for the phone. Looking down at the screen, she smiled and, whispering, said, 'Goodnight, Alex.'

He would know that she had seen it — *know that I've heard him.* And, ultimately, that was all that mattered. In a world of expectation, *and ridiculous, wince-worthy dad jokes,* that was what he needed. *Someone to listen to him.* She wanted him to know — *to realise* — that she could be that person. *And that I'm not just another Robert telling him what to do and who he has to be.* Silent, steadfast, centring, she could be the ruby at the centre of his compass. And so, she was not so much punishing him, but showing him, to prove that she was.

# The Crystal Ladder Society

*On a dreary March evening, in between Act II and III of The Homestead, Mary and her father attend a historic meeting of The Crystal Ladder Society.*

Ernest Stansfield had been an impressive baby. Large, with big, handsome, hazel eyes, he always seemed to be looking at everything — pupils wide — as if for the first time. Regarded as an early sign of his cerebral prowess, everyone told his parents that he would grow into them — only later did they realise that their infant son's ocular grandeur was due to the fact that the muscles in his irises were almost always contracting, struggling to focus. Hyperopia. And so, for as long as he could remember, Ern had worn eyeglasses.

Even so, Philip and Jayne Stansfield's eldest child still proved an intellectualist. A born academic, professorial even in toddlerhood, for whom elegant cursive seemed to have come more naturally than tying shoelaces, he was also abundantly animated. His chronic bespecklement did little to temper his energy and so, as a boy and, later, a young man, Ern thrived in social situations. Gregarious, an easy conversationalist, he could talk to anyone about anything. Some termed him extroverted. Others, less enthusiastic, a chatterbox. Regardless, his intrinsic agreeableness, and distinct, loud laughter, did much to win him friends, resulting in a social circle quite a bit larger than he could manage. By the time he reached adulthood, he had thus been forced to winnow the grain, meaning that he spent most of his time with a select handful of companions. Attendants of the same university, they had affectionate nicknames for each other. There was Hippocrates, Pliny, Antinous and Cato. He was Pythagoras. In time, their friendship was formalised into a fraternity; a meeting of minds intersecting art and science, politics and economics, enamoured by Classical civilisations. Inaugurated one dreary Thursday evening over Port and vanilla ice-cream in Ern's top-floor college room, he named it The Crystal Ladder Society.

To be a member of The Crystal Ladder Society was to uphold the principles of gallantry and good taste — and that necessitated, strictly, no female attendance. However, it was a well-known fact that, shortly after starting his second year of university, Ern had fallen under the influence of a certain fine art student. Fine, because the art was suitably old and pointless, but also because she herself was such. Tempestuous, as fiery as the colour of her curls, she demanded, as proof of commitment, to be allowed to attend one of Ern's — so she called them — queer little meetings. After that, the standard slipped, and Cato seemed to bring a different girl every week. Even so, membership remained a male prerogative, until, eventually, having earned his doctorate and relocated to a different university so as to teach economics, Ern reestablished

The Crystal Ladder Society as a fraternal organisation for students with an interest in the original founding principles of gallantry and good taste. Now, on yet another dreary evening, the society was celebrating its thirtieth anniversary.

'I greet thee, Demosthenes! It's good to see you don't mind the drizzle!'

'I greet thee in return, Pythagoras! And, no, no — not enough to keep me away tonight.'

Ern, warmly gripping the other man's hand, welcomed him out of the rain and down the steps into the basement.

A spacious room in one of the buildings belonging to the university's economics faculty, eclectically furnished with squashy velvet sofas, heavy oak cabinets, and a charming, but dysfunctional, Black Forest cuckoo clock, it was reserved every Wednesday and second Sunday for the society's meetings. Given the occasion, the basement room was currently especially decorated. Seasonal foliage, beeswax-dripping candelabra, and a miniature marble Nike of Samothrace, carried, heavily and mindful of the wings, from Ern's upstairs office to the meeting room earlier in the day. The evening's attendants were likewise embellished. A collection of men uniformly dressed in formal attire and gold masquerade masks, they each wore a black, knee-length robe over their evening jackets, their individual patternings — from coloured trims to elaborate pleating to embroidery on the gowns' bell-shaped sleeves — representing the wearers' respective colleges. The only one of the gathering not to be wearing an academic gown was, coincidentally, also the only female in the room. Heeled-shoes and layers of black silk tulle. And so, the brotherly bond had been violated once again: Mary was, after all, her mother's daughter.

'I see you didn't bother selecting appropriate footwear for tonight, Cleon,' Mary said, tilting her head down in the direction of the shoes worn by the young man she had just approached. Black, with white velcro straps, vent perforations and red soles, they were rowing shoes.

'I came straight from training,' the young man retorted, voice vitriolic. 'Remembering the mask was absurd enough.'

Unblinking, Mary made a small, scoffing sound. 'I think it's an improvement,' she said. 'It covers half your face, after all.' To that, the young man snorted and, moulded gold plastic over his eyes and nose, shook his head. Mary was already walking away. Her own mask was made of gold lace. Fringed from ear-to-ear with white pearls, a delicate chain hung from under each down to her chin, resulting in a shimmering veil of gold that caught the light each time she moved her head.

There were more young men only a few paces away. First year students, they had taken the corner of the room, chuckling, cocksure, but not so much so as to compete with their older and more demonstrative fellows. One or two offered a subdued 'good evening' to Mary as she passed them by. She said nothing, continuing onwards.

There was a stout, broad-shouldered man at the drinks' table. Pouring himself a glass of brandy, stooped and balding, he taught particle astrophysics and cosmology at the university.

'I greet thee, Heraclides.'

A broad smile and the masked professor turned to face

her. 'Hypatia! I greet thee!' Leaning forward so as to hold her by the shoulder, he placed a kiss on her cheek.

'Has Pythagoras seen you?'

A sip of brandy and the man called Heraclides shook his head. 'Not yet.'

Looking away from him, Mary quickly scouted the room. Spectacles over his mask, her father was beside the Nike of Samothrace, in boisterous conversation with a group of doctoral students. As if sensing her, Ern momentarily turned from the group and, raising his head, smiled across the room at her.

'He enjoyed your last paper,' she said, eyes still on her father.

'On the compression of dark-matter clumps?'

Mary, turning back to the masked man, nodded. 'Yes,' she said. 'He thinks that it—' she paused and, considering, narrowed her eyes. 'Means something.'

The professor erupted into laughter. 'Well,' he chuckled, 'I would hope so! That paper represents twelve months of research.'

'Quite,' Mary nodded. 'Not to mention a routine risk of armageddon.'

More laughter from the masked professor. 'Non-hazardous collision events are entirely ordinary in the universe, Hypatia.' A wide smile and he took a drink from his glass. 'You and I've had this conversation before.'

Mary smiled. 'So we have.'

The professor offered a chuckle. 'Don't you worry about it.' He reached to pat her on the arm. 'We men of science must be bold in the pursuit of knowledge.'

Poised, the smile remained on Mary's face. 'I must leave you and those other clever men to continue pursuing it, then.' Gold and the lustre of pearls. The masked man nodded happily. Mary gave a demure dip of the head, then, stepping away from him, added coolly, 'Enjoy your evening — and playing God — Heraclides.' Glass to his lips, the professor chuckled into his brandy as he watched her move away.

She was walking to one of the other tables when she felt a hand on the small of her back.

'Good evening,' a voice whispered into her ear.

'Good evening,' she said back, smiling, twisting so as to face her newest masked companion. Keeping his hand in the same position, it skimmed the smooth silk of her dress, slipping around her back, her waist, to her front, settling over her stomach as she turned.

'I hope I'm not late,' he said, holding her.

A hum, but still smiling. 'You'll do.'

'You look beautiful.'

Smile widening, she gave a laugh. 'You'll do.'

He laughed with her at that. 'You know,' eyes moving, he glanced the room, 'I didn't expect all of this.'

She turned so as to look with him. *Wine goblets. Candelabra. Daddy's winged Nike.* A slow, teasing smile and she turned back to him. 'All of what?' she asked.

Laughter, and he tapped his finger against her stomach. 'You know what,' he said. 'The dim lighting, the masks—' hand moving, he slowly touched her lace-covered face. 'The—' another pause and his voice changed, louder, laughing slightly, 'the, quite frankly, disturbing all-male attendance.'

Mary laughed and leant into his touch. 'Jealous?'

'Is it always like this?'

She continued laughing. 'Not the masks, but certainly—' her lips twisted as she pushed her face towards his, 'the all-male attention.' A slow, provocative smile and she laughed. 'Apologies, I mean attendance.'

Chuckling, he shook his head. 'Wonderful. That makes me feel so much better.'

Her smile was wide, filling his vision. 'I imagine so.'

He kissed her then, laughing. Pushing their fingers together, he gave her hand a squeeze, pinching the tip of her thumb before releasing her. Lips still parted as he pulled away, she sighed. *Oh, Alex.* A long, damp afternoon train ride, he had made the journey specially for her.

'Would you like me to get you a drink?' Alexander asked, again looking around the room. Mary nodded. Before he was able to do so, however, they were approached by a middle-aged man in an offensively elaborate masquerade mask. Dress code gold, but encrusted with purples, reds, blues and greens, it looked to have come straight from a Venetian carnival — some three hundred years earlier. He walked well, his shoes a deep emerald green; his jacket, velvet, the very same colour. Despite his rich plumage, he was, however, in keeping with the meeting's other attendants in so far as he was wearing an academic gown. Black with pleats, Alexander immediately recognised it as being similar to his own.

'I greet thee,' the man smiled, offering his hand to Alexander to shake. 'Cato.'

Alexander, nodding, introduced himself in return. 'Alexander.'

'A pleasure.' The maverick mask-wearer's voice was clear

and bright. Still smiling, he moved his hand to Mary. An intake of breath and he said, 'Child of Aphrodite.' He grinned widely. 'You must be Mar—'

'Hypatia,' Mary interrupted, shaking his hand. 'I greet thee.'

The man, Cato, burst into laughter. 'Hypatia!' Eager hand-shaking and he held her. 'Of course! How splendid! I greet thee!' More laughter, he continued to hold her hand. 'Although,' long, enunciated syllables, 'historically, female membership—'

'Formally,' Mary interrupted, 'I am an honorary male.'

This caused the bejewelled man to laugh all the more. Energetic, theatrical guffawing and he exclaimed, 'Exquisite! And, it is only fitting!' He was still holding Mary, his left hand having joined his right in the course of their conversation so that he was now cupping hers in both of his. 'Fitting, truly.' He sighed then, his laughter dying. A second sigh and he looked at Mary more thoroughly, his bright, blue eyes moving over her face from behind his mask. 'You should know,' the man said to her, his voice lower than before, 'that I loved your mother.' Yet another, softer, sigh. 'But—' laughing now, he released Mary's hand, 'there was only one man Francesca loved. Speaking of whom—' twisting on the heel of his emerald shoe, Cato looked about the room, 'where is the old stallion?' Loud, joyful laughter when he saw him. 'Pythagoras!' he shouted across the room. Upon hearing him, Mary's father, animatedly engaged in a group discussion, immediately turned in his direction. Grinning, and Cato beamed, before offering a polite smile to Mary and Alexander. He excused himself and strode towards Ern. 'Pythagoras! My old, dear friend, how I greet thee!'

Standing together, Mary and Alexander watched the two men embrace each other, thoroughly and with hearty affection.

Alexander turned to Mary. 'Was that—?'

Nodding, she said, 'Yes. It was.'

Alexander started laughing. 'But, he's really famous!'

'I know!' An excited smile pushed itself across Mary's face.

Alexander, laughing still, shook his head. His eyes returned to the two men laughing with each other on the other side of the room. Back-slapping and infectious chortling that could have only been provoked by youthful remembrance. Alexander turned again to Mary. 'Who is your father?' he grinned at her.

Giggling, her head shaking also, she simply said, 'I don't know.'

Once their laughter had subsided, Alexander again asked if she wanted a drink. 'Or,' he said, looking at her, 'would Hypatia rather something else?'

Seeing his expression, Mary gave a short laugh. 'It's my society name. Hypatia of Alexandria.'

Alexander was smiling. 'Of Alexandria?'

'Yes,' Mary nodded. 'She was—'

'I know who she was,' Alexander interrupted with a laugh. Grinning, and he touched her chin. Mary kept her eyes on his. A slow, prying gaze and he said, 'I'll get us drinks.'

She watched as he left her for the drinks' table. Posture elegant, eyes big and brown, hair thoroughly touchable, *and stubble recently shaved*, she loved to look at him.

'My love—' Her father's voice made her turn away. 'Look, Hypatia, look who it is!'

Reaching to take his hand, Mary stepped towards Ern. 'I know, Pythagoras,' she smiled softly. 'He and I have already spoken.'

At her father's side, Cato dipped his head and smiled at her.

'Perfect,' Ern beamed, nodding as he held his daughter's hand. He was wearing a brown herringbone twill bow tie with matching waistcoat, his eyeglasses still, somehow, balanced on top of his mask. 'I had no idea he intended to come tonight,' he continued, looking from Mary to his friend.

'I wanted to surprise you,' Cato said, smiling warmly at Ern. 'Besides,' he added, glancing at Mary, 'I'm on hold until next week. The studio's practically down the road.'

'True, true,' Ern agreed, nodding. 'Even so, it's ever so nice — especially for the younger members.'

Cato chuckled. 'Historic. Although,' he looked at Mary, 'I warrant your father is considerably coy about this society's origins, Hypatia.'

Ern was laughing. Before either man could offer anything more, however, Alexander returned with his and Mary's drinks.

'I got you this,' he said, passing a small glass of ruby red liquid to her. 'I couldn't find anything other than strong alcohol.' She thanked him and, with a small sniff, accepted the drink.

'I say—' it was Ern, eyes narrowing as he, clearly confused, looked at Alexander, 'you shall have to forgive me, but I cannot place you. It's—' with a waft, he gestured to his own face, 'the mask, you see.'

Mary looked from her father to Alexander, at first stunned,

then, suddenly, brightly, giggling. At her side, Alexander slowly responded, 'It's Alexander.'

Opposite, Ern, still scrutinising him, began to nod. 'Ah,' he said, 'I greet thee, Alexander the Great.'

Mary's giggling increased. 'No, Daddy,' she chastised, the gold chains dangling from her mask glinting as she shook her head. 'It's *Alexander*.'

Next to her, Alexander offered a small smile. 'Yeah,' he said to Mary's father, 'the not-so-great one.'

At that, Ern erupted into guffawing laughter. 'Goodness!' Leaning back, closing his eyes, he held onto himself. 'I'm so sorry, Alex!' More stomach squeezing laughter and he choked, 'I didn't know you were coming! Hypatia never—'

'It's alright,' Alexander said, likewise laughing as he shook his head. Mary, still giggling, was holding his arm.

Cato, meanwhile, was struggling to catch his breath. 'Do you need a new prescription for your glasses, Pythagoras?' A demonstrative clear of the throat and he slapped Ern on the back. 'Mask or not, even I can see he's Hippocrates' boy. He's his duplicate!' Then, gesturing to the glasses of fortified wine in Alexander and Mary's hands, 'He even shares his sensitivities!'

Ern was consumed with laughter. His hand resting on Cato's shoulder, he nodded in breathless agreement. Then, struggling, again apologised to Alexander.

'Gosh,' Cato exclaimed, gripping his friend, 'do you remember, old boy, that time he got upset with us about the absinthe?' Ern, loud, guffawing, back-slapping, had his eyes squeezed shut. Cato, continuing, turned to look at Mary and Alexander. 'I prayed,' he told them in clear, clean words, 'agonised, even, for him to kill me.' A pause for a suitably oxygenated laugh. 'Instead,' he continued, 'all he did was look at me with those big, brown, disappointed eyes.'

Mary was grinning. 'What did you do?'

'Cato, here,' it was her father, chuckling still, but ability to enunciate restored, 'introduced Alexander's mother—' he turned to look at him, 'to the green fairy.'

Sudden swelling laughter and Cato retook the conversation. 'It was not just I!' Chest puffed, he placed a hand to his velvet jacket. 'Antinous! Pliny! Cesca! Even you, Pythagoras!'

Mary's father was breathless again. Alexander, listening, watching, was shaking his head in disbelief.

'Oh, Alexander,' Cato said to him, reaching to lay a hand on his shoulder, 'you mustn't think poorly of your dear mother.' Laughter and, eyes wild blue, he patted the younger man. 'She didn't know.'

'I don't see how that improves the story,' Mary said, grinning.

'No,' Ern laughed. 'It certainly doesn't.'

Cato, chuckling, shook his head. He turned so as to smile at his friend. 'That's because you must explain it properly, Pythagoras. You see,' an exuberant gesture and he returned to Alexander, 'it was one of your mother's rare,' a pause and he stressed, '*unchaperoned* visits.'

Ern was laughing again.

'Your father—' Cato's smile, wide and white-toothed, locked on Alexander, 'you understand, I love him, I'd die for that man,' a dramatic snap of his fingers, 'in a heartbeat, but—' more loud laughter, 'he is a prude, Alexander, and he kept your mother — sweet songbird that she is — locked inside a cage, safe, even from himself.'

Ern, wracked with mirth, reached for Mary's hand, struggling to stand upright. 'You're cruel, Cato,' he said, shaking his head at his friend.

The other man held up his finger. 'But, correct! Correct, Pythagoras!' More laughter and he passed the conversation back to Ern.

He was holding Mary to him. Chuckling, he looked from her to Alexander. 'Your father,' Ern explained, 'had a supervision with one of his professors. Sophie was visiting — she and Rob were recently engaged — and so we promised—' he paused to give space to Cato's chortling, 'we promised to care for her whilst he was gone. It was only an hour or so, we just had to keep her company, but—' another pause for yet another burst of laughter, 'but,' Ern continued, 'when he got back—' he trailed off at that, his words smothered by gasping guffawing. Held tight in his arms, Mary was giggling.

Cato stepped in to carry the story. 'Your mother, Alexander,' he said, blue eyes on brown. 'She has a beautiful singing voice. Truly angelic.'

Ern was still laughing. Even so, he — winded — forced a breath and reached for Alexander. Summoning momentary calm, he said to him, 'You know she does.'

Alexander, gripped by persisting disbelief, could only nod in agreement.

'And,' Cato continued with a flourish, 'she is that rare variety of person who — sweet, graceful, pure — becomes all the more so when they are intoxicated. Perhaps, then,' a broad, spirited grin and he looked at Ern, 'it is no wonder that Hippocrates was ever eager to keep her locked away from us.'

To that, Ern could only laugh and shake his head. In his arms, Mary was overwhelmed. Giggling, breathless, happy, she loved her father, loved Sophie, loved Robert, and so loved hearing stories about them all together. Turning her face from her father's waistcoat, she looked at Alexander. He was, albeit reluctantly, caught in laughter also. Eyes on his, Mary smiled widely at him.

'Oh my goodness! Look who the cat dragged in!' Blue eyes flashing from the gathering to the door, Cato brought his hands together in a sudden, gleeful motion. Ern, Mary and Alexander turned to look. Cato had already stepped away from them. 'My kith!' he exclaimed, extending his arms to the man who had just entered the room. Retreating tufts of black-grey hair and a gold mask like all the others. Grabbing him, Cato drew him to his chest so as to be able to kiss the top of his balding head. 'My kin! My brother! I greet thee! How are you, dear Pliny?'

Laughing, the man shuffled out from his arms. 'I greet thee, too, Cato. I am well, thank you,' he said, smiling. 'How are you?'

Cato was elated. 'Glorious!' Still holding onto him, he directed him towards the others.

Ern reached to pat him on the arm. 'I greet thee, Pliny,' he said as the new man moved to stand beside him.

'I greet thee, Pythagoras,' Pliny returned, nodding. 'Sorry I'm a bit late — there's a good reason for it, though.' He was holding a shopping bag and raised it, wafting it at the group.

The sound of glass bottles contacting each other and Ern chuckled.

'What a noble soul you are, Pliny,' Cato grinned, slapping him on the back. 'And, impeccable timing. We were just discussing alcoholism — and its deplorability.'

Lively laughter, and Ern shook his head. Next to him, released and now standing with Alexander, Mary was smiling softly. Similarly smiling, Pliny turned to her and, with a dip of the head, bid her greeting.

'I greet thee, too, Pliny,' she said, matching his nod.

The man with the black-grey hair turned to Alexander next. Stepping forward slightly, Alexander held out his hand to him. 'Good evening, Professor.'

A growing smile and the older man took his hand. 'It's Pliny tonight,' he said, gripping him warmly. 'And you—'

'Right,' Alexander nodded. 'Of course,' still nodding, 'And, um—'

'Alexander,' Mary offered. Then, grinning, 'The Great.'

At that, her father and Cato cackled with joy. Laughing with them, Pliny reached to pat Ern on the arm before asking where he should put the alcohol.

'We'll show you,' Cato interrupted, wrapping his arm around the other man. 'I shalln't let you out of my sight tonight.' He paused and turned to Ern. 'Either of you. Come!' And so, the three of them as one, they moved away towards the drinks' table, leaving Mary and Alexander standing alone together.

'That was surreal,' Alexander said once they were safely out of earshot.

Smiling ear-to-ear, Mary looked at him and shook her head.

'I shall never look at any of them the same again,' Alexander continued with a laugh.

Matching his expression, Mary pushed her arm through his. 'They gave your mother absinthe,' she giggled.

'And they might try the same with us tonight if we're not careful.'

Still giggling, Mary rested her face against his shoulder. 'Prude,' she teased.

Laughter and Alexander squeezed her. 'Don't,' he said. 'You know I'm not like my father.'

Her face still against his shoulder, all Mary could do was laugh.

Shortly afterwards, it was time for the meal. Masked and gowned, the society's members took their seats, Pythagoras, Cato and Pliny at the table's head, Hypatia and Alexander down the other end. Baskets of bread and bowls of soup were carried into the room by black-waistcoated attendants. Two carried the wine, lifting bottles from trays so as to pour portions into eager glasses. There was chattering as they did, masculine voices intonating along the length of the table, soup steam filling the air. When every place was occupied by a bowl, the head of the table rose from his seat and invited calm. Like the sound before it, silence blanketed the table.

'*Benedic, Domine, nos et dona tua*,' the society's masked leader enunciated. In the candlelight, many of the members dipped their heads and drew their hands to prayer. '*Quae de largitate tua sumus sumpturi*.' Loud, clear words. Some were muttering along with him. '*Benedicentes sanctum nomen tuum*, *pro Fundatricibus nostris caeterisque Benefactoribus, quorum beneficiis hic ad pietatem et studia literarum alimur.*' A moment, a breath, and the head of the table continued, his voice quieter than before, '*Et concede vivis gratiam et requiem mortuis. Per te Dominum nostrum. Amen.*'

'*Amen,*' the rest of the table uttered in unison. With that, Pythagoras returned to his seat. Grace said, the eating — and talking — could commence.

'Of course, we cannot be certain that they are Pythagorean. Their existence simply cannot be confirmed prior to the fifth century. To say otherwise is nonsense.'

'Rubbish.' Leaning forward, soup spoon in hand, a young man, masked with fine, blonde hair, directed his speech at the previous, dark-haired speaker. 'There are plenty of suggestions that the verses were known as early as the third century BCE.'

A snort and the previous speaker flicked a hand in the other's direction.

'Hierocles of Alexandria—'

'Not contemporary—'

'Irrelevant,' the blonde speaker reclaimed. 'His commentary enjoyed great popularity for a great many centuries. He presented the verses as Pythagorean. As did Proclus of Laodicea.'

To that, the dark-haired young man laughed viciously. 'Now that is bunk,' he said, holding his spoon out in front of him. 'A poor Arabic translation of disputed attribution is hardly gospel.'

'I wonder—' a new entrant to the conversation, clear-voiced and straight-postured, held a wine glass to her lips, 'what difference you think it makes, Cleon.'

The original speaker turned to look at her. Others at the table, slurping soup and sipping wine, were on the edge of their seats, gladly listening to the unfolding argument.

'At this point,' Mary, still holding her glass, continued, 'the verses are Pythagorean — regardless of actuality.'

Several seats away, the blonde young man nodded, happy to have found reinforcement.

'Precisely,' another — older and wider — agreed. 'We cannot afford for them to fade away. And a firestorm of pseudo-intellectualism obsessed with puritanism and origination is a surefire way to condemn them to obscurity.'

A line of masked faces, there was much nodding. Further along the table, others, previously out of the loop, were being drawn into the debate.

'What are we discussing, gentlemen?' someone, face concealed by a glittering gold mask, asked.

The blonde young man leant forward in his seat. 'The Golden Verses of Pythagoras, Themistius.'

At the head of the table, Ern, hearing his society name, turned his head in the direction of the discussion. Seeing him, Mary smiled and shook her head. 'Not you, Pythagoras. Your namesake.'

'Ah,' Ern said, smiling. 'Very good.'

'Modern life is too crowded, too showy.' It was the older, wider, speaker. 'Pythagoras teaches a simple, spiritual beauty. Much needed succour in the twenty-first century.'

Alexander was using a chunk of bread to wipe the last of the soup from his bowl. Following the conversation, head moving from right to left, he pushed it into his mouth and waited for the next to speak. Attention having been captured, it was Ern.

'It is not merely spiritual beauty, Polybius,' he said, smiling as he did. 'But how it relates to the physical. For example—' pushing up the sleeves of his gown, he straightened himself in his seat. The rest of the table was quiet, captivated, listening. 'Verse eighteen speaks of physical calamities — disease, poverty, loss — and how one ought navigate them. "Support your lot with patience, it is what it may be, and never complain at it." These,' Ern explained, eyes sweeping the length of the table as he did, 'are very physical things, with very physical consequences. Sickness, starvation, homelessness, grief. A spiritual remedy alone is not enough. And so, supporting one's lot must encompass practical — physical — virtue too. Patience being a physical demonstration of spiritual virtue. The act, for example, of reflection taught in verses forty through forty-five.'

The other man, Polybius, nodded and said, '"Never allow sleep to close your eyelids, after you went to bed, until you have examined all your actions of the day by your reason."'

'It's our interaction with the physical universe,' Ern continued, nodding. '"In what have I done wrong? What have I omitted that I ought to have done?" And,' looking around, he smiled at some of the younger members seated at the table, 'of course, important, "if you have done any good, rejoice."' He was nodding and his eyes, big and bright, momentarily settled on his daughter at the other end of the table. 'Such wisdom,' he explained, looking elsewhere, 'that conscious splitting of experience, acknowledging the rational, but also the irrational, the physical and the spiritual — that there are two realms — is why great thinkers like Pythagoras have done so much to advance humanity.' A small laugh and he reached for his wine glass. 'Life can only be explained in rational terms up to a point. Yet, equally, we would be foolish to ignore rationality in favour of absolute spirituality.'

His students were silent. At his side, Cato moved to place a hand on Ern's arm. 'You are very wise, Pythagoras.' His words were full and sincere. Others, quietly mumbling, slowly began to nod, absorbed, absorbing, still meditating on all that had just been said, finishing their soup.

'Are you okay?'

Mary looked up from her bowl and smiled at Alexander. 'Yes,' she nodded. 'Thank you.'

A reciprocal smile and he slipped his hand under the table. Knees touching, he caressed the top of her leg. 'Your father's surprised me tonight,' he said, eyes on her.

Mary turned again from her bowl. 'He has?' she asked.

'Well,' a grin, 'he did admit to spiking my mother with absinthe only half an hour ago. Plus,' laughter now, 'he wasn't able to recognise me with a mask on.'

Mary was giggling. 'That's true,' she said, lips twisting into a smile. 'But,' quieter, her smile softened, 'he is brilliant.'

Alexander was watching her. 'Yes.' He nodded, then squeezed her gently under the table. 'He is.'

Mary didn't immediately turn away. Soup spoon in her hand, she could see her smile reflecting in the warmth of his eyes. *I love you.* Some days she worried he would never say it back. Silent, the table animated around them, Alexander kept his hand on her leg as he watched her eat the remainder of her soup.

The second course was *filet mignon*. Pan-seared and served with *béarnaise* sauce, creamy mashed potatoes and abundant *Cabernet Sauvignon*, after many weeks away from home at university, Alexander expressed how happy he was to eat proper food. Simple, and yet luxuriously creamy vanilla ice-cream followed, then, a selection of fine cheeses, and, finally, a glass of pudding wine. By the time the final course was being cleared away, many of the party were drunk — on both food and alcohol — with the evening thus determined a success.

'I hope I don't have to be responsible for him,' Alexander said, sitting with Mary on one of the basement room's squashy sofas, gesturing in the direction of Pliny. Gleeful, giddy, he was standing by the drinks' table, arm-in-arm with Ern and Cato. Alexander shook his head. 'Make sure he gets to the station okay.' Her cheek resting against his chest, Mary laughed. An early morning lecture scheduled for the next day, Alexander — along with his professor — would be taking the night train back to university after the meeting.

'It's always so embarrassing,' Alexander continued. 'And the masks and the names make it more so.' More than a little tipsy himself, he breathed in the scent of Mary's hair as he spoke to her.

Giggling, she shushed him. 'Don't insult us.' With her hand, she touched his mouth. 'This society is very old, and has many *famous* alumni.' More giggling and they both looked across at Cato.

'You told me it was lame.'

Scoffing. 'It is lame.'

Alexander laughed and pushed his nose into her curls

again. 'You seem to enjoy it,' he said, words muffled by hair. 'Hypatia.'

She was giggling.

He would have continued to hold her, but a voice summoned them from across the room.

'Great one!' Then, louder: 'Alexander!'

Alexander and Mary shuffled themselves upright on the sofa.

'Come hither!' Cato called again. His arm was extended, index finger, long and elegant, beckoning for them with a hurried, hooking gesture. At his side, Pliny and Mary's father awaited, each holding a glass of Port, eagerly chortling.

'We must enlighten you as to your origin,' Cato said to Alexander as he and Mary moved to join them. 'How—' a deep, dramatic pause and he opened his arms, 'you came to be more than mortal.'

Ern and Pliny were still laughing. Alexander, quietly looking on, was confused. 'I think he means Alexander the Great,' Mary said, addressing his befuddlement.

'Indeed,' Cato continued, arms as wide and expressive as his smile. 'Your legendary journey to Siwa!'

At that, Ern, chuckling, with eyeglasses still balanced overtop his masquerade mask, stepped forward and placed a hand on the younger man's arm. 'As you know,' he said, grinning, 'Alexander the Great was a hero and a conqueror. The world fell before him. He would defeat armies that outnumbered him as many as ten to one, sweeping through the Balkans, Anatolia, Syria, Phoenicia — south into Egypt.'

'That,' Ern continued after a quick sip from his glass, 'was where he founded Alexandria in 331 BCE. Before then, however, he went on an expedition into an isolated part of the desert, some five hundred treacherous miles west of Memphis, to the Siwa Oasis, specifically to consult the Oracle of Amun.'

Eyes and hands brightly animated, Ern was fixed on Alexander as he spoke, unaware that others had begun to gather on the fringes of his story-telling.

'There,' he explained, 'Alexander experienced a so-called "mystical death".' Ern paused and smiled. 'The journey was dangerous, you see, but, more than that, it was, well, spiritually revelatory, for, when the high priest of the shrine greeted the young conqueror, he is said to have conferred upon him divinity — not merely the flattery due to him as a foreigner liberator or pharoah, but the proclamation that he, Alexander of Macedon, was the son of Zeus-Amun.'

Here, Cato again opened his arms widely. 'The son of a god,' he announced theatrically.

'Quite,' Ern nodded, bespeckled visage buoyant. 'And, as the son of a god, and yes a living god himself, Alexander was informed that the empire of the world had been reserved for him. That he would have dominion of it — all of it — as was his divine birthright.' Eyes on Alexander, he was beaming through his glasses. 'You see, Alex,' Ern chuckled, head inclining towards him, 'men like Alexander the Great can be thought of as vehicles of spirit, agents of chaos or creation — both maybe — who have the ability to metamorphose the consciousness of an entire generation. Why, of the entire world, even.'

Around them, it seemed as though nearly every member in the room had gathered to listen. Aside from the slight clinking of drinking glasses being brought to lips, bumping against gold masquerade masks, there was no sound other than Ern's voice. He continued:

'Just as a great artist or musician may use their genius to craft a masterpiece that alters the flow of culture, so may an agent of fortune bring change — the only difference being,' he nodded his head as he spoke, 'that their influence is further reaching, all-encompassing and, above all,' glass still in hand, he raised a finger, 'sanctioned by the divine.' A pause, and Ern took a drink. 'It is the intervention of the cosmic mind that means these people — these vessels of spirit — need not be initiated into a mystery school or the like. The divine element is, after all, with them from birth.' His eyes were twinkling and he chuckled generously. 'Do you understand what I'm saying, Alex?'

All attention in the room now turned to Alexander. Standing in front of Mary's father, his hand on the side of his face, he nodded, slowly, and said, 'I think so.'

Breathlessness, then there was overt laughter, with Cato, the sleeves of his emerald velvet jacket pushed up to his elbows, stepping forward so as to wrap an arm around the younger man. 'Of course he does, Pythagoras! He is the great one!'

Ern's chuckling increased at that, with others in the room likewise indulging in laughter. At Alexander's side, Mary was giggling.

'But,' it was Cato still, 'you omitted the crucial part of the tale.' He was looking at Ern. 'The ram's horns.'

'Oh!' Mary's father exclaimed, laughing. 'Quite right!'

Caught in Cato's embrace, Alexander looked from one man to the other. 'The ram's horns?' he asked.

'Why, yes,' Ern said, nodding at him. 'The horns of Amun — the god from whom Alexander acquired divinity.'

It was Pliny's turn to speak now. 'They're a symbol of supremacy. Of the god himself. Alexander took to wearing them after the oracle's revelation.'

Slow, confused nodding and Alexander's eyes moved back to Ern. 'That's how he asserted his divinity,' Mary's father explained. 'In coinage. In ceremony.'

'And—' Alexander's eyes moving again, it was Cato once more, 'that,' the elaborately-masked man continued, 'is how you shall assert yours.' A sudden, energetic movement and he released Alexander so as to step into the middle of their gathering. Smiling widely, he gestured to the drinking glasses in his friends' hands. 'Finish up, gentlemen — the oracle must make a proclamation!' Abundant laughter, and Ern and Pliny drained the last of the Port in their glasses so as to pass them to Cato. Suitably empty, he took one in each hand, then turned so as to face Alexander. 'You have no need for initiation,' he said to him, his eyes wildly blue. 'For you are the great one!' With that, and to the sound of laughter and loud ovation across the room, Cato raised the glasses and held them against Alexander's head, along his hairline, above his temples — mock ram's horns, an inebriated offering to the god Amun.

'Now,' Cato declared, still holding the glasses against his head. 'Go on and conquer the world, Alexander!'

The room seemed very happy about that and immediately erupted into, even louder than before, joyous, drunken cheering. Admittedly, he was not one of their own, not a formal member, not even — Mary smiling at his side — an honorary formal member, but he was, more widely, their man. Alexander, for his part, was utterly embarrassed, but did his best to nod and smile at the greatly enthusiastic, bejewelled, mask-wearing performer who stood in front of him.

'Thank you,' he managed, nodding. 'Thank you.'

Cato lowered the glasses shortly after that, still smiling, still laughing, discarding them on the nearby drinks table. 'You are a triumph, Alexander,' he said to him, his eyes sparkling as he caught those of the younger man. 'I am very glad to have met you tonight.'

Alexander, softly laughing, nodded his head and admitted the same. 'It has certainly been a night to remember,' he smiled.

Next to him, Mary was grinning. He turned to look at her then, and she could see — *in the soft, brown centres of his eyes* — that he was drowning in introspection. A giggle and she reached for his arm, holding onto him with both hands.

'I'm here,' she said to him, moving so that her mouth was close to his ear. The room was loud as, all around them, the others splintered into fresh conversation. Opposite, Pliny — her father and Cato on either side of him — said something about a man he had seen on the train earlier that evening.

Mary spoke into Alexander's ear again. 'Thank you so much for coming.'

His hair tickled the side of her face as he nodded. A smile and he turned to her again. He placed a gentle hand on her waist. 'Thank you for inviting me,' he whispered. *Big, brown, hopeful eyes*, the inner voice was quietening.

Mary nodded in return. Hands high up his arm, she was still clutching onto him. It made her so happy to see him — *to have him* — and so she giggled again, turning her head to look about the room as she did. Her father, jolly and brilliant, was watching her. In that second, they caught each other's eyes and she smiled at him. He offered her something in return, a smile, *half a smile, a conflicted attempt at one*. It was just a wobble, but once started motion and gravity demanded follow-through. Abruptly interrupting Pliny's story, Ern excused himself, mentioning something about using the bathroom. His strides were long as he hurried to exit the room.

'I should go after him,' Mary said, eyes and words faltering. Releasing Alexander, apologising, for herself and perhaps her father also, she rushed to the door.

'Daddy.' Lifting the skirt of her dress, she quickened along the corridor that led to the stairs. The gold chains of her mask swung about her face. 'Daddy.' He was just ahead of her. 'Stop, Daddy.'

He did as she said and turned to look at her. Glasses and mask pulled from his face, he was crying.

'Oh, Daddy,' Mary said. Immediately, and with her whole body, she reached for him. Arms extended in return, she felt the air rush from her lungs as he held her.

'I'm sorry, my love,' Ern apologised, mouth pressed to her hair. 'I'm so sorry.'

'Don't,' she said back, her hands caressing his back. 'There is nothing to apologise for.' Shaking, she could feel tears on her face.

A moment to breathe her in, then, slowly, but still holding

onto her, he took a step back. Eye-to-eye, they looked at each other.

'It simply took me by surprise,' Ern explained to his daughter. 'Reminded me—'

'You don't have to explain, Daddy,' Mary whispered, nodding, smiling softly.

Ern mirrored her expression. 'You know—' a pause, a breath, he continued, 'You know, your mother used to call these meetings queer.'

More tears on her face and Mary laughed. 'That's because they are queer, Daddy.'

Her father chuckled at that, then, inhaling deeply, pulled her to him again so as to kiss the top of her head. Breath unsteady, eyes squeezed shut, Mary made herself small in his arms.

'Where have you wandered off to, Pythagoras? I thought I told you that I shalln't let you out of my sight tonight.' Laughter and Mary, sniffing as she did, pulled away from her father. Cato and Pliny, eyes and smiles wide with warmth, were walking down the corridor towards them. Once they reached them, Cato patted Ern on the shoulder.

'You seem to have lost your mask, old friend,' he said, grinning. 'You ought to be careful, someone might recognise you.'

More laughter and Ern, grinning also now, returned his mask to his face. 'Thank you, Cato,' he said, nodding.

The other man offered a delicate shrug. He turned to Mary then. 'And,' he said, 'what are you doing here?' A slow smile and she gave a laugh. His grin was ridiculous.

At his side, Pliny was smiling also. 'Go on,' he said to her, nodding. 'We'll look after him.'

'Certainly,' Cato added, again patting Ern on the shoulder. Mary looked at her father. Still sniffing, but smiling, he nodded at her.

'Go on!' Cato continued, louder and with more exuberance than Pliny. An exquisite green velvet arm was wafted in Mary's direction, shooing her. 'Return to your Alexandria, fair Hypatia!'

She giggled at that, taking a step back as she did. Cato again wafted his arm in her direction, laughing this time. Another step back and she looked one final time at her father, before turning to walk back along the corridor, the sound of happy laughter behind her all the way to the door that led to the room where Alexander was waiting for her.

# Apotheosis

*Alexander makes another Friday evening journey home from university. That night, Mary waits for him. A misunderstanding the following morning is captured in The Homestead's Chapter Thirty-Seven.*

It was past midnight. The house had been quiet since ten. Sophie had played Chopin's *Prelude Op. 28, No. 4* on the piano, Robert falling asleep on the sofa, a difficult week of work and a final cup of tea — *cinnamon, chamomile, rooibos, and lemon balm* — tipping the balance between waking and slumber. Soft, heart-wrenching, hauntingly beautiful music, Mary had very almost fallen asleep herself. They bid her goodnight soon after that, Sophie tweaking her nose as she walked from the piano to the sitting room door. One of her father's old economic books balanced across her knees, Mary had moved to sit on the other sofa. The curtains had not been drawn and so she had a clear view of the driveway.

She heard him before she saw him. Tyres crunching over gravel, *and old rusted metalwork, bitten by the salt from the sea, clanking against the exhaust pipe,* he was quicker to turn off the engine than usual. Abandoning her book, not long finished, on the sofa, she hurried outside to greet him.

'I've missed you.'

'I don't ever want it to be Monday.'

'Don't think about that now.'

Then everything was plunging. Legs out from underneath her, it was breathless, burning incandescence. Hands and lips and laughing, brighter than the Moon above them, they struggled for each other and for air. Then, an act of clairvoyance and he carried her up the steps to the front door. She just about managed to close it behind them as he walked them through it.

'I've missed you,' he said again, pulling away from her, rubbing his nose against hers as he did.

In his arms, her back now pressed to the wall, she nodded. 'I've missed you too,' she whispered.

Keeping her against the wall, he returned for more kisses. Softer than before, slowly pulling at her bottom lip, he breathed into her, opening her, his breath sweet and warm on her tongue. That perennial feeling, an instinctual yearning for connectedness that only the other could satisfy, and he pulled her away from the wall, carrying her still, hands on her back and on her bottom.

'Alex, don't.' Muffled giggling and she clung to him as he nudged the door to the sitting room open with his boot and transported her to the sofa. Then, an effervescent sound and she giggled some more. 'The carpet, Alex.'

Setting her down on the sofa, Alexander looked at his feet. 'Shit,' he whispered. He took a step back. The faint outline of dirty footprints on the carpet and, looking back at Mary, he started laughing also.

Propped against the cushions, she looked up at him and grinned. 'Your mother will kill you.'

A wider grin. 'I don't care.' He came back to her then. Scrambling to kick his shoes off, he pushed her into the cushions of the sofa, climbing on top of her, holding her there, kissing her, breathing her, running his lips down the length of her neck, making her giggle and ache for him.

*It's nothing like they say.* Alexander's body pressed against her own, Mary could feel their lungs rise and fall together. *It's so much more than they say.* Ineffable, a utopic feeling, paradisiacal and paradoxical, she was utterly captivated. Colours, those of the midday Sun and lavender flowers *and soft strawberry marshmallows*, and she sighed as he kissed her. She had no control over it, and had no desire to develop any. She was in love.

A creak from upstairs made them stop. Muffled giggling into the sides of each other's necks, they held each other on the sofa.

'I thought they were asleep,' Alexander hissed into her ear. More muffled giggling and she squeezed her eyes shut as she clung to him. Breaths held and bodies still, his hand was inside her underwear. Struggling to suppress their laughter, they waited for the sound of the toilet flush. A minute and they heard it, and then another creak as the person upstairs walked back to bed. Silence restored, they both, expelling breath through their nostrils, started giggling. He returned to kissing her after that.

Fingers in his hair as he tasted the skin behind her ear, Mary encouraged him to look at her. 'Take me to bed,' she whispered, searching for his face.

Grinning, Alexander adjusted his position. 'I rather like the sofa.'

She shook her head. 'Take me to bed.'

Eyes on hers, he held her, then, lowering himself so that they were nose-to-nose, gave her a single, long kiss. 'Okay,' he whispered.

With that, he raised himself off her and stood. Giving his hands to her, he led her from the sofa to the hallway. In silence, they climbed the stairs to her bedroom together.

Through the door and blind, instinctive caresses led them to the bed. Shrugging clothes from bodies, they found each other in the dark of the room. Softly, he stroked her face, reminding her that she wasn't alone in slow, smooth, soothing motions.

*Hold me.*

A touch of the body and they quickly became each other, melding to one singleness in the centre of the bed.

*Love me.*

Lower and deeper, and deeper still, falling from a height to an even higher place, the sensation was exquisite. It wasn't just physical, but metaphysical — an abstract and yet entirely palpable feeling which caused everything to fall away. The world was smaller than it was, its troubles insignificant; she only needed him, for in him he carried a piece of her, a shard of herself that was cosmic and divine, and through reunification with it she achieved apotheosis.

*Create me.*

Soul gasping, she allowed the ethereal piece to find her, for it to wash over her and scintillate her spirit. Her hands were on his back, his tangled in the curls of her hair. Moving inside of her, he kissed her, murmured to her, coaxing her to cry back. Swirling softness, parting, a sudden melting wave, and then, quivering, for an ephemeral, timeless moment, she forgot her body and became the stars.

He joined her soon afterwards, locating the piece of himself that existed in her. Guiding his face with her hands, she watched it happen. Then, naked skin wet with sweat, he lowered his lips to hers and kissed her. 'I've missed you,' he said softly.

Looking up at him, eyes wet, she nodded back.

He rolled off her after that, collapsing into the pillow next to her. Soft, shallow breathing, he reached for her hand. Fingers together, they didn't say anything more. There was no need. *We are the same.* After that, slowly, her face beautified by tears, she felt herself start to slip away, contented, whole, falling asleep.

# The Sentinel

*Over the course of several weeks, Mary recovers from the injuries sustained in The Homestead's climactic and concluding chapters.*

She had fallen asleep again.

'Mare—' Whispering. 'Wake up.'

Squinting. Croaky. 'Sorry.'

Head shaking. 'No.' A soft smile. 'Don't say anything.' He touched her chin. 'Just try to stay awake. If only for a bit.'

Nodding and she focused on his face. Eyes. Wide. *Concerned.* She smiled and pushed her hand across the pillow to find his. Another soft smile and he took it. Thumb. Knuckles. 'Do you want me to get you anything?' Slow. She shook her head. Eyes. *Concerned again.* 'I should ask him about the dose.' He looked away from her then, searching. Short, shallow breaths. He came back to her. 'Let me help you.' Reaching. Hands raised. Pillow. He brought it to her chest. She shook her head. 'You have to, Mare.' A gentle hand on her back. *Pain.* He encouraged her to lean into the pillow. 'You have to.' Soft. 'Just ten.' Eyes. *Pleading.* 'Ten deep breaths, then you can sleep again if you like.' Slow. Eventually, a nod. He held the pillow to her chest and counted. 'One.' *Pain.* 'And breathe out.' Eyes closed. 'Two.' *Pricking.* 'That's good. Slow and deep, Mare.' He was holding her hand. 'Three.' Pillow. 'And out.' *Pain.* 'Now another.' Tears. 'And out.' One dripped onto the pillow. 'Five.' Fingers. Squeezed. 'You're halfway there, Mare.' More finger squeezing. 'Six. You're okay. This will help, I promise. Seven.' She was trying. 'Deep breath for eight.' Splintered. Coughing. Hushing. His hand moved. 'I've got you.' She was braced against the pillow. 'I'm here.' Throat. *Burning.* 'Have a drink.' Eyes. *Concerned.* He put the glass to her lips. 'Just a sip. You're okay.' The coughing lessened. He was holding her hand again. 'That's enough for now.' A small smile. 'We'll do it again later.' Another smile. *Encouraging.* 'You're doing good. It's good you cough.' Hand squeezing. 'To clear your lungs.' Leaning back against the sofa. Pillow. Blanket. *Soft.* 'I love you.' Slow. Smile. 'Sleep again now.' A nod. Eyes. *Real.* She let hers close then. Next to her on the sofa, he would stay and watch.

As it was, Mary had been taking oxycodone for two days. Liquid opioid pain medication, Robert had prescribed it to her after the previous painkillers had failed to manage the pain of her fractured and bruised ribs. It had been six days since the fire and, although she had borne the suffering uncomplainingly, as the days dragged on it was clear that she wasn't going to be able to do it alone. Five millilitres every four to six hours, she was drowsy and confused — but comfortable.

'Are you sure the dose is correct?' Carefully closing the door to the sitting room, Alexander stepped into the hallway. His father had just come through the front door.

'Good morning to you, too, Alex,' Robert said, smiling.

His son took a deep breath.

'I explained this yesterday,' Robert continued, stepping around Alexander so as to be able to reach down and untie the laces of his shoes. 'The first couple of days require adjustment.' Pausing, he looked up at the younger man. A smile and he said, 'She's fine.'

Arms crossed over his chest, Alexander forced a nod. Behind him, there was noise on the staircase. Turning, both he and his father watched Ern walk down the stairs.

'Good morning, Rob. Good morning, Alex,' Mary's father smiled.

Robert said good morning back. Alexander, arms still folded, simply nodded.

'So,' Ern said, concluding the final step so as to stand on the hallway rug, 'how is she this morning?' He looked from one man to the other.

'She's sleeping,' Alexander answered, gesturing towards the sitting room door.

'Ah,' Ern nodded, 'that's good, I suppose.'

Stepping forward, Robert placed a hand on the other man's shoulder. 'It is, old friend,' he said. Then, smiling, 'I'm sure she'll be awake in a bit so you can sit with her.'

Unsure, but smiling, Ern gave a nod.

'In the meantime,' Robert, turning, looked at his son, 'I would appreciate your help with—'

'Can't do it,' Alexander interrupted. 'Sorry,' he added. He dropped his hands to his side. 'I need to make sure she has her next dose and—'

'Ern can look after her,' Robert interrupted back. Gentle, brown eyes and a wide smile, he turned back to his friend. 'Can't you?'

Ern's face brightened. 'Of course!'

'He can help you instead.' Both men looked at Alexander. His arms were once again folded across his chest. 'Then there's no need for me to explain her medicine or anything like that.'

Standing together at the bottom of the stairs, Robert and Ern were quiet. Then, nodding, Alexander's father said, 'Okay, then.' He looked at his friend. 'Is that alright with you?'

Ern, slowly, nodded. 'I suppose so.' A small smile and he pushed his glasses further up his nose. 'Do you, er—' shaking his head, he smiled at Robert, 'need me to bring anything, Rob?'

Chuckling, Robert put a hand on his friend's shoulder. 'No, no,' he smiled, patting him. 'Just your hands.'

'Oh—' grinning, Ern chuckled also, 'perfect.' With that he nodded at Robert and Alexander, then quickly gestured towards the kitchen. 'I'll get a cup of tea first.'

'A wonderful idea,' Robert smiled. 'I'll join you.' He turned to his son. 'Alexander?'

Alexander stood still beside the sitting room door. 'No, thanks.'

His father nodded. 'Okay, then.' A smile. 'Well, I'll pop back up later to check on Mary.'

'Do,' Alexander said, nodding.

A final smile from his father, then he and Ern turned towards the kitchen. Continued, cheery conversation and Alexander watched them go before turning to reenter the sitting room.

Upright on the sofa, a thick, white woollen blanket tucked around her, Mary was in a deep sleep. Sweetly sonorous, her breath was rhythmic, each exhale making a slight snoring sound as it was expelled through her nose. Careful not to disturb her, Alexander pulled the pouffe across the carpet so as to sit down on it in front of her. Her hair was combed back, secured in two braids on either side of her face. A strand or two had escaped, and he watched as they moved, lifting from her face, disturbed by her snoring exhalations. Slowly, he reached to tuck them behind her ear. Unstirring, unaware, she continued to sleep.

***

Black and blues. There was a firecracker nearby. 'It's like New Year's.' She didn't know who spoke, but thought it might have been herself. Somewhere else. Lost in the blue.

'Hello?'

There was smoke. Trails of grey in the trees, the leaves were dying. Yellows, reds, and browns. Floating underneath her, they carried her like a river, a current of crinkled death that pushed her deeper into the woods.

She didn't want to be here.

Now there was a bird in a tree. Black, with enormous, cold, blue eyes. A shriek and it flew from a leafless branch towards her face. Hands raised to protect her eyes, she screamed in silence. When she uncovered her face, he was standing there in front of her.

'How did you get out?' That voice again. She touched her lips, confirming her own mouth was silent. Slowly, he grinned at her.

Another firecracker. This time she saw the explosion. A sudden flash of white somewhere in the distance and the trees had leaves again. Still, there was death underfoot — brown, wilted, moulded mulch, specks of white and red. Blood. Chest bare, he was moving towards her. Ground shaking and she fell and reached for the death, fingernails full of it as she dragged herself away from him. He was already on top of her.

'I'm going to enjoy my meal.'

The smoke was pluming now. Grey turned to black and she couldn't see anything. Panic, and she felt so very afraid. Her legs were trying to run, but she was on the ground, in the mud, in the death, and the smoke was inside of her, thick dark plumes of poison that took the very life from her. She couldn't breathe, she was being chased, her legs wouldn't stop moving, even though she was on the ground. She couldn't breathe. She couldn't breathe. She was on the ground. The poison was filling her.

'Mary.'

Jolting, she woke. A pair of gentle brown eyes and she immediately reached for his hand.

'It's okay,' he said, softly drawing her to him. Pain in her back and chest, but she needed him. 'It's okay,' Alexander repeated. 'It was just a bad dream.'

Silent sobbing. Mary nodded. Gripping him, her fingers burrowed into the fabric of his shirt.

*It was just a bad dream. It was just a bad dream.*

She squeezed her eyes closed. Short, shallow breaths.

*It was just a bad dream.*

'It's over now.'

***

The board was almost full. The top left corner, however, enticing, with its easily accessible triple word and double letter squares, was hers for the taking — if only she could conjure a word.

'Do you have anything?'

Next to her on the sofa, eyes and words soft, Alexander was waiting for her to direct him. Looking between her and her letter rack, he offered her a small smile. Opposite, sitting on a chair brought in from the dining room, her father was quiet, thumbing the side of his face as he examined his own letter rack. The pouffe, and Guinevere seemed to be having similar trouble. On the other sofa, however, Robert, Sophie at his side, was still and smiling, clearly eager to play his next word. Shaking her head, Mary dropped her eyes to her letter tiles.

*A - B - E - F - H - K - N*

*Plus the 'Y' on the board.*

Eyes back to the Scrabble board, she returned to the top left corner. 'Year', placed by her father the previous turn, provided her with an opportunity. *Bridge off the 'Y' and the triple word is yours.* She looked again at her letter tiles. *Four letters. Five with the 'Y'.* At her side, Alexander was likewise studying them.

'You know—' Mary looked up. It was Robert, *still smiling.* 'If you cannot come up with a word,' he continued from the other sofa, 'you could always swap your letters out and skip a turn.'

A chuckle, and her father looked up so as to grin at his friend. Mary, shaking her head, tapped the back of Alexander's hand. Grinning also, he tilted his head towards hers. Lips to his ear and she whispered, 'I have a word.'

Alexander looked at his father. 'She says she has a word,' he grinned.

The same smile and Robert laughed a little.

'Mummy—' fiddling with her tiles, it was Guinevere. 'Is zeet a word?'

Sophie looked across at her daughter. 'I don't think so, bumblebee.'

A sigh and Alexander's sister returned to her letter rack. Mary glanced at her as she did. *'Z' near the end of the game.* A small, satisfied smile and she returned to her own tiles. As she did, she noticed her father was cleaning his glasses. White and purple polka dots, he was polishing them with a handkerchief.

*Hanky.*

Mary's eyes dropped to her letter rack. A quick glance at the board and she tapped Alexander's hand. When she whispered the word to him, he smiled. 'Okay,' he nodded, reaching to take the required tiles from her rack. Following her instructions, he placed them on the board. As soon as his hand moved to the top left corner, there was sighing from Robert. Watching, Mary flashed a smile at him.

Ern was calculating. 'A base score of fifteen,' he said. 'With a double letter on 'K', so twenty. Then, tripled, sixty points.'

'Well done, marshmallow,' Sophie beamed from the other sofa. Another smile, this one softer, and Mary dipped her head in her direction.

'A good score,' Robert conceded, smiling across at her. Alexander's sister — *lamenting her 'Z'* — was less than pleased, but offered reluctant congratulations all the same. In the far corner of the room, sitting in his armchair, Robert Senior sniffed. 'Didn't think hanky was a proper word.'

Turning to him, Sophie tutted. 'Of course it is.'

'It's handkerchief,' the old man grumbled.

Sophie tutted again. 'Be quiet, Robert.'

Dictionary in hand, the younger Robert looked at his father. 'It's informal, but it's in the dictionary,' he said, wafting the book towards the old man in the armchair, 'and therefore perfectly acceptable.'

On the other sofa, Alexander turned to grin at Mary. Silent laughter and she shook her head.

Two weeks had now passed since the fire. Healing, but not yet recovered, Mary had adjusted to the medication, could breathe deeper with each new day, and was starting to look more herself. Bruises — to her body and to her face — had largely faded, being but a light brown where they had once been purple and swollen. At their ugliest, they had been a sickly yellow-green colour, the one on her face, from where the metal door had knocked her unconscious, being the most repulsive. Her ribs still hurt, one broken, but the drugs helped to mask the worst of the discomfort. It was her voice, however, that caused the most irritation. Warned not to strain her vocal cords before they were fully healed — the smoke and the strangulation having swollen and scorched them terribly — she was trying to make the best of an aggravating situation.

Robert was placing his letter tiles on the board.

'Do you need me to get you anything, Mare?'

Turning, Mary smiled at Alexander and shook her head.

*He never leaves me alone.* Which was, in many wonderful

ways, a good thing. And yet, once in a while, it was an aggravating situation also.

'I've just remembered—' looking across at her, it was her father, 'the university museum has a new exhibit next month.' Eyes turned in his direction, Mary was listening. 'Japanese weapons,' Ern nodded, smiling. 'They're showcasing a whole load of them. Samurai swords—'

Mary tapped the back of Alexander's hand. '*Katanas*,' Alexander said.

'Yes,' Ern continued, again nodding at his daughter. 'And those spears—' pausing, he waited for Mary to tap Alexander's hand again.

'*Yari*,' the younger man said. Another whisper from Mary and he added, 'For *Sōjutsu*.'

In his chair, Ern chuckled. 'Yes, of course — *Sōjutsu*!'

Mary, smiling, encouraged her father with a nod.

'Well,' Ern carried on, 'I thought it might be nice for you to go and see them and—'

'Perhaps,' Alexander interrupted. Next to him, Mary was still. 'It's a bit much for now, though, isn't it?' Everyone else was quiet. Eyes on the other man, Alexander's leg was bouncing up and down, foot tapping the carpet. Mary shuffled on the sofa. A quick tap on the back of his hand and she encouraged Alexander to look at her. Eyes, searching. Then, a soft shrug and she smiled. *It's okay*. She squeezed his hand. *Don't smother me*.

Slowly, a smile in return and his leg went still.

Watching from his chair, Mary's father nodded. 'I'm sure they'll be an opportunity,' he said, looking at them both. 'Whenever you're ready.'

Mary, nodding, gave him a smile. Next to her, Alexander did too, quietly offering a word of agreement. After that, it was Guinevere's turn to place her letter tiles.

Mary hadn't yet had the chance to ask Alexander about that day. Pain and discombobulation, *not to mention the frustrations of actually speaking*, it had gone unspoken. Besides, he was so determined to take care of her — *a sentinel ever on the edge of slumber* — that she was quite certain he would have rebuffed any attempts to refocus the conversation. She had heard it mentioned, *one time, when they thought I was sleeping*, that Robert had had to stop him from going into B Building. *I don't think he would have come back out unless he found her, my darling.* Then, there was the blood: he had already been covered in it before he pulled the trigger on the bull.

'We shall have to arrange to go shopping once you're better, my marshmallow,' Sophie smiled from the other sofa, leaning forward and extending a hand in Mary's direction as she did. Carefully, Mary shuffled in her seat. A quick squeeze of the younger woman's fingers, then Sophie released her. 'I want to get some new slippers,' she added, beaming. 'The satin ones are just so pretty.'

Next to her, Robert looked from his letter rack to his wife. 'I thought you bought a new pair only a week or so ago, my darling.'

Giggling, Sophie shook her head. 'Not *those* sorts of slippers, my dear.'

Listening, Mary was grinning.

'Oh,' Robert said, a smile widening on his face. 'I see.'

Across from him, Ern was rearranging his letter tiles,

preparing to place them on the board. 'Slippers, Sophie?' he asked, eyes focused on the game.

More giggling and Sophie nodded. '*Ballet* slippers,' she said.

Ern started laughing. 'Ballet?' He looked across at her now. 'I didn't know you did ballet.' Straightening his glasses, he laughed again.

Sophie turned to Mary now. 'Marshmallow,' she said, voice and expression bewildered. Opposite, the younger woman, head resting against Alexander's shoulder, was laughing silently. Again glancing up from his letter rack, Robert offered a small smirk.

'You haven't told him?' Sophie continued, protesting.

Ern, Scrabble tiles in hand, continued laughing. 'Haven't told me what?' He looked from Sophie to his daughter.

Sophie's eyes moved to him. 'About our ballet classes.'

Guinevere, Alexander and Robert were laughing now too. A quick moment to compose himself and Robert looked across at Mary. 'Mary,' he said, a smile on his face, 'surely you've told your father?'

Rolling her head to Alexander's ear, Mary whispered to him. Laughter, then Alexander said, 'She says it's too embarrassing.'

Arms across her body, Sophie was immediately grieved. 'Embarrassing?'

More whispering. 'Not you, Mother.' Careful not to disturb Mary too much, Alexander leant across to the other sofa. Smiling, he took his mother's hand in his and — although she seemed momentarily despondent — raised it to his mouth to kiss her. 'She just says it's very girly, that's all.'

A meek mumble and Sophie nodded. Everyone else in the room was chuckling.

Back with Mary, Alexander's ear was once again close to her lips. Message received, his laughter increased. 'But most of all,' he said, looking first at Sophie and then at the rest of the room, 'it's embarrassing because she enjoys it.'

At that, the laughter — most especially the guffawing from the armchair in the corner — increased, with Mary turning her face so as to hide it against Alexander's shoulder.

'Well,' Robert said, addressing his wife, 'I love that you love ballet,' a pause and he, grinning, looked across at Mary, 'both of you.'

The laughter continued. In his chair, Ern smiled, shaking his head. 'You should have told me, my love.'

Face still against Alexander's shoulder, Mary was laughing. Alexander grinned and held her hand. Ern was finally able to place his word after that. 'Coat', it was a simple scorer — *no special squares, six points* — which, with the letter bag now empty, left him with only four tiles.

Mary was once again studying the game board.

*B - E - E - F - M - O - S*

She was feeling tired and her chest hurt. Using an 'E' that was already on the board, she instructed Alexander to play 'beef', earning her a modest nine points. Like her father, she was left with four tiles for her next turn.

Whispering to her now, Alexander asked if she was okay. Slowly, she pushed her lips to his ear. 'Tired,' she said.

He nodded and, holding her, ran his thumb across her knuckles. 'It'll be time for your medicine in half an hour,' he whispered back. Mary nodded and, eyes closing, rested her head back against his shoulder. Opposite them, Robert was playing his turn. Thirty-two points, he used all but two of his letter tiles.

She couldn't remember what became of her last letters. The next she knew, the tiles were being collected up off the board and returned to their bag. Reaching across from the other sofa, Sophie took her letter rack from her and, opening the little drawer on the game cabinet, slotted it away with the others. It was a beautiful board. *Alex. Christmas.*

'Well done, marshmallow.' Sophie was talking to her. Soft eyes, there was a smile on her face. 'You won.'

Mary nodded. Then, turning, slowly, she looked for Alexander. He was still with her, his hand over hers as he helped his mother tidy the game away.

'I should go down and check on her.' Head, turning, Mary looked for the voice. Robert was standing. His eyes were on his watch. 'It really could be any moment.' Sophie was nodding. Her father's chair was empty. 'I don't want her to be alone.'

'Okay, my dear.' The drawer was closed. 'Do you want some help?'

At Mary's side, Alexander was shuffling. She didn't want him to go. An arm around her middle, he was encouraging her to sit forward. *Don't go.* He was starting to stand now. Then, soft, a breath on her ear. 'Come on,' it said. 'I've got you.' Tired, eyes closing, she nodded and let herself be moved. Her back and chest hurt — *pain* — but she stood up from the sofa. Short, shallow breaths. It would be a difficult climb up the stairs, but he would help her. Tucked in bed, pain medication and pillows, he wouldn't leave her. *Sentinel.* And so, holding onto him, she smiled.

***

She almost slipped on the rocks. Seaweed and broken seashells, the shore was lined with debris. Strong, sharp salt air. Rumbling. The waves were crashing. Light fading in the sky, a seagull moved above her. There was a compass in her hand, but he wasn't there.

Red at the centre, the needle pointed forward. More wet rocks and she turned from the water. Overhead, the seagull squawked, wide wings white, and followed her into the trees. She wasn't wearing any shoes and the ground was gritty, seashells having penetrated the woodland floor, getting caught in between her toes.

'Where are you?'

The needle swung to the left. More trees. The light was fading fast. On the ground, water was starting to seep up through the soil, and she could hear the sound of waves still. Above, the gull was gone, and so was the Sun. Darkness. The sea was up to her ankles now.

Then, a scream, and she could see a light in the distance. Orange and red. Needle swinging, the compass told her to go towards it. Rising panic, water knee-high, she pushed through the sea and the trees.

'Is that you?'

The compass was gone now. Her hands empty, she held onto the forest and pulled herself through the water.

A gap in the trees and she found her way out. Wet grass,

the waves were retreating into the woods. Then, ahead of her, she could see the habitation buildings. A and B and C and the Seat. It was nighttime, but she could see everything clearly, the Moon above big and bright, red and orange.

There was a figure in the distance. Pacing the grass, they were holding something in their hands. At their feet and in the grass, there were shadowy shapes.

'Alex?'

Bits of broken shells in between her toes, she continued forward. The Moon was bigger than before and it painted everything red.

'Alexander!'

He turned to look at her then. A shotgun in his hands, his face was covered in blood. 'I'm sorry.' Brown eyes big, his words were warped. He gestured towards the shapes in the grass with the gun. 'I didn't mean to do it.'

Looking, she realised they were bodies. The water was back again, lapping at the bits and pieces, floating, leaking blood.

He was standing in front of her now, the Moon full and red above him. 'I didn't mean to,' he said again. A sob and, the shotgun in his hands gone, he was reaching for her. There was blood all over him. Hands on her arms and he cried, 'I just had to digest my feelings.'

Mary opened her eyes. Quiet, propped up against a mound of pillows, her eyes slowly adjusted to the light in the room. She saw that he was sitting next to her on the bed. Legs crossed, a book open on the quilt in front of him, he was eating a sandwich. When he realised she was awake, he turned and smiled at her. 'Are you okay?'

Nodding, she slowly smiled back at him. A delicate clear of the throat and she whispered, 'You?'

Putting the sandwich down on the plate, Alexander shuffled closer to her. A wider smile and he said, 'Of course.' Gently, he rubbed his nose against hers. 'I've got you.' He kissed her then, a soft contact on her lips. Pulling away from her, he searched her face and smiled again. 'Do you need anything?'

Mary shook her head.

'Do you want to sleep some more?'

She shook her head again.

'Okay,' he nodded, smiling. He looked back towards the book on the bed. 'I can read to you, if you like?'

A nod this time and so he picked up the book. Repositioning himself so that they were side-by-side, resting together against the headboard of the bed, he tucked her against him and opened the book, turning to the right page so as to read her a story.

***

'It doesn't have to be a long walk.'

'I'm okay, Alex.'

'Even so—' a playful smile and he led her into the hallway, 'it doesn't have to be long.'

He insisted upon putting her shoes on for her. White canvas espadrilles, with wedged heels and delicate ankle buckles, he sat her on the bottom step of the stairs, crouched before her, pushing them one at a time onto her bare feet. His family in the other room, it made her feel silly to be so fussed over, but, it was his birthday, and so there was nothing that she could say to stop him. Besides, it was the first time she had made any effort with her appearance in weeks, and so — as silly as it was — it also felt good to be appreciated.

'Wait here whilst I put mine on,' he instructed, touching her leg as he stood. A moment to slip on his own shoes and he came back for her, taking her hands in his so as to help her stand.

He told her that she looked beautiful. She reminded him that it was his day, and that she ought to be the one saying nice things to him. 'After all, I didn't even get you a present.'

Laughing, he touched her lips. 'Can you stop bringing that up?'

She pulled a face, then, laughing too, kissed his fingers away.

It was the final week of June and Mary was all but back to normal. Voice restored, bruises healed, pain medication no longer necessary. She was, however, still under strict orders — *Alex, Daddy and Robert, and in that order* — not to over-exert herself. Heavy-lifting was a 'no'. Ballet and *Taekwondo* could wait. As for helping with the daily chores of the homestead, that was utterly out of the question. *Now, I cannot even put my own shoes on.* A small smile and, looking at him, she squeezed Alexander's hand.

They were outside, crossing the gravel driveway to the lawn which the front of the house overlooked. A fence, then a sloping sea of green and the grass melted to vines. Before that, a small, white gate opened onto a path which led to one of the island's many vantage points. Alexander led Mary through it, then closed it behind them.

'I thought you might like to see the sea,' he said, turning to look at her as they walked together. A soft smile and she nodded. Six weeks of rest and, despite being on an island, the furthest she had managed was the vegetable garden and back — the water always just out of sight.

'We could go swimming if you're up for it.' He was grinning, teasing, and so she nudged him with her elbow. A laugh and he feigned injury. 'Your strength really has returned.'

'And so has your ridiculousness,' she said, elbowing him again.

Another grin and he drew her closer to him, continuing to guide her along the path towards the lookout.

The ground was grassy, speckled with tiny white flowers, blue-violet blooms and the vegetated tops of rocks pushing up from the cliff below. There was a flat patch in the middle with an open view of the sea, and on it a picnic blanket had been arranged. Light blue, and spread with cushions and plates and a little vase of flowers, there was also a wicker hamper and cooler box. Mary was surprised to see it.

'It's lovely,' she said, turning her eyes from the blanket scene to Alexander. 'But how?'

A shrug and he grinned. 'A birthday present.'

Mary, grinning too, nodded and again looked at the picnic.

He was eager to sit her down. Leading her to an empty space on the blanket, nudging a cushion closer to her so that she could lean against it, or hold it to her, whichever she preferred, he afterwards began unpacking the food. 'I'll do it,' he said, stopping her with a smile as she leant forward to help him. Soft brown eyes, then he looked away, fingers lifting tin foil from around sandwiches and the other things his mother had prepared for them. The salty smell of the sea, and a breeze blew up and over the edge of the cliff, ruffling through his hair and then hers as she watched him arrange it all onto plates.

'What would you like first?' he asked as he lifted the lid off a tub of strawberries.

A smile and she told him to choose for her. After taking care of her for so many weeks, *and so thoroughly*, she had come to appreciate just how important a sense of purpose was for Alexander. *He needs to be needed.* And so, restless, devoted, *and thus on occasion overbearing*, he was at his best when he had it — and floundered when he didn't.

'Thank you,' Mary said, taking the plate that he passed to her. Strawberries and a slice of cake, they were starting with sweets.

'I admit,' he said, grinning as he settled on the blanket next to her, 'I don't really know all that's in here—' a laugh and he shuffled so as to peer inside the cooler box.

'Knowing Sophie, everything, I should imagine,' Mary replied, smiling as she raised a strawberry to her lips.

A grin. 'That's true.' Then, looking at her — *for a split second, strangely* — he added, 'It really is good you have your strength back then, so as to be able to eat it all.'

Chewing, Mary nodded and watched him do the same.

At some point in time — *I don't know whether it was that day, that moment, or some other moment in the days since* — Alexander had started looking at her differently. It wasn't a bad differently, *at least I don't think so*, but rather a novel sort of apprehension, *an inner fidgeting*, that made her think he must have realised something that he ought to have known a long time ago.

*Not that he loves me.* A smile and Mary, eyes on his, brought another strawberry to her mouth. It was something else. *Perhaps that I'm mortal.*

It was silly — *like him putting on my shoes* — a laughable and conceited thing, *even to think*, but something that she suspected all the same. As children, climbing trees and swimming in the sea together, she had always been the more rough-and-tumble of the two of them. He had never broken a bone, had cried the day they found a clutch of baby birds, dead, outside by the back door. She hadn't even cried the day her mother died. Of course, she had cried afterwards, *and he had been there for me when I did*, but he had never looked at her any differently. *Not like everyone else.* She was still a tree-climber and a sea-swimmer. *Still the one to tell Robert about the dead birds.* In many ways, Alexander's innocent, unchanging opinion of her had acted as an anchor point from which her love for him had grown.

*And now he sees me differently. A little less strong, a little more human.* Of course, maybe he always had seen her like that — maybe he was just better than everyone else at hiding it. Even so, 'please don't pity me,' she said, thoughts tumbling through her lips.

Surprised, Alexander put his plate down on the blanket. 'Pity you?' A smile and he shook his head. 'I don't.'

Sighing softly, Mary put her plate down next to his.

'What makes you say that?' he continued, watching her.

She shook her head. 'I just don't want you to pity me.' Her

words were low and slow and caused Alexander to breathe deeply.

'How could I pity you?' he asked. He reached for her then, taking her hands in his. 'You're the strongest person I know.'

Eyes on his, she didn't blink. Both of their legs crossed beneath them, Alexander shuffled across the blanket so that they were sitting knee-to-knee.

'You are, Mare,' he continued, smiling at her. 'You're stronger than I am — without a doubt.' He laughed at that and squeezed her hands. Eyes wide and for him, her face softened as he did. 'I admire you so very much,' he said to her. 'I love you.'

Mary nodded. 'I love you, too, Alex.'

Softly, moving his hand to her chin, he pulled her to him for a kiss. Then, even softer, said, 'I've always loved you.'

A slow smile, squashed between his thumb and forefinger, and Mary shook her head. 'That's a lie.'

Alexander shook his head in return. 'It isn't.'

Mary laughed.

'I'm serious,' he said, also laughing. 'It's not a lie!'

Still laughing, Mary shook his hand from her chin. 'Really? Do you want me to cite occasions?'

More laughter. 'Please don't.' Then, taking her hands back in his, he said, 'Allow me to explain.'

Quietening, a grin lingering on her face, Mary nodded, then readjusted herself against her cushion.

'So,' Alexander said, passing Mary's plate of cake and strawberries back to her, 'a very long time ago, there was a little girl and a little boy, and—'

A laugh. 'Sorry—' Another laugh and Mary put her hand

to her mouth so as to guard against cake crumbs falling onto the picnic blanket. Swallowing, she looked at him. 'Are you still talking about us?'

Alexander was grinning. 'Look,' he said, lifting his own slice of cake to his mouth, 'this is only possible if I explain it like this.' A bite and, pausing, he started to chew. 'That way—' mouth full, he hurried to swallow. 'That way,' he repeated, grinning at her, 'I can at least pretend I'm talking about someone else.'

Listening to him, Mary laughed, then signalled for him to continue.

'As I was saying,' Alexander said, 'there was a little girl and a little boy. They would do all sorts of things together. Ride bikes. Play games. Read books. Everything. Even things they shouldn't have. Climb fences and—'

'And get stuck on the wrong side of them.' Mary was smiling.

Alexander, smiling also, nodded. 'Get stuck on the wrong side of fences.' A quick laugh and he bit the end off a strawberry, its red juice dripping onto his chin. Swiping it away, he continued, 'They did everything together. They—' he paused and reached to touch her chin, 'were best friends.'

Eyes wide, Mary nodded.

'And,' sighing, Alexander's hand dropped to his side, 'it probably could have stayed like that forever. Only, one day, something happened.' He looked at her as he spoke, his words darkening. 'The little boy was, well, slowly — although perhaps he didn't realise it at the time — slowly changing, changing from being a little boy to something else. It was a summer's day when he realised it — or, at least, started to realise it. The sun was shining and so they went to swim in the sea. All of them — the little boy and the little girl and their family. There was ice-cream and sandwiches and they even convinced their grandpa to drag out the little, old boat they sometimes used when the water wasn't too choppy.'

'I remember this,' Mary said, listening to him.

Slowly, Alexander nodded. 'Well,' he continued, 'the little boy really liked playing in that boat. He really liked swimming in the sea. He—' a pause and, eyes dropping for a second, Alexander cleared his throat. Slowly, he looked up at Mary and said, 'He really liked the little girl too. Only—' Still looking at her, he paused again. 'Only, the little boy's grandpa saw just how much he really liked the little girl and said something to him that — considering he was, underneath it all, still just a little boy — was really not something that he should have said.'

Mary's voice was quiet. 'What do you mean, Alex?'

Clearing his throat, Alexander shuffled on the blanket, straightening himself. 'The details aren't important,' he said, voice clearer than a moment before. 'But, it was inappropriate. In many ways.' He kept his eyes on hers. 'He shamed the boy for how he felt — for feelings he didn't fully understand or really even know he had. And,' Alexander shook his head, 'not only that, he told him that — even if he did feel those things he only half-understood — that they weren't really his feelings to have, but rather ones that had been put there, by him, by the little boy's father, and,' Alexander's eyes were unmoved from Mary's, 'by your father, too.'

Quiet, Mary put down her plate and reached for Alexander's hand.

'And so,' Alexander continued, voice reduced once more, 'because of what his grandpa said, the boy decided he didn't want to feel those things he had been made to feel. He wanted to feel something else. Something that was his. And that took him to places he never should have gone. Places he never really wanted to go. Places that made him feel even worse about himself than his grandpa had ever made him feel.'

Still holding his hand, Mary nodded and, barely audible, whispered, 'Oh, Alex.'

Hearing her, Alexander squeezed her fingers and, with a deep breath, pushed a smile onto his face. 'But— and this is important,' he said. 'Whatever the ridiculous, wicked old man said—'

Opposite, Mary laughed.

Laughing too, Alexander continued, 'Whatever he said to him, whatever ridiculous, wicked old man things he said to him, it was still the little boy's fault.'

Reaching, Mary put a finger on Alexander's lips.

'No,' he said, kissing her fingertip. 'No.' Hand-in-hand, he squeezed her. 'Because the little girl never did anything wrong. She never tricked him into feeling anything. Never conspired with the adults. She was just a little girl.'

'And you were a little boy,' Mary said, shaking her head at him.

'To begin with,' Alexander replied, holding her eyes and her hands. 'But I wasn't always. I grew up. I could have changed how I was with you. Let go of what Grandpa said.'

'But you did, Alex,' Mary said, shuffling closer to him. 'You did.'

They were both quiet then, still and silent, looking at each other. Sea air and soft breeze, a bird flew over them. Eventually, his voice quiet, but strong, Alexander said, 'You're my best friend, Mary.'

Nodding, eyes wide and full, Mary replied, 'And you're my best friend, too, Alex.'

They reached for each other after that, leaning together, still crossed-legged on the picnic blanket, heads resting on each other's shoulders, wet with tears and longing. 'I am so honoured by you,' Alexander said to her, both laughing and crying as he held her. Her hand moved to the back of his head, gripping him, any and all her words lost to emotion, overwhelmed by his embrace. A moment longer and then, gentle with her, he gave her a soft squeeze and let her go.

'There's something else,' he said, sniffing. A smile and he turned towards the wicker picnic basket. Wiping the tears from her eyes, Mary prepared herself for what was to come next.

'It's from a gift shop in town.' Grinning, laughing, he pushed the object through the air towards her. Sketches of starfish, the sorts of scientific illustrations synonymous with oceanographers, the journal was thicker than when she had seen it last.

Crying again, Mary simply asked, 'Why?'

'Just look inside,' Alexander replied, laughing, encouraging her to do so with the touch of a hand. A nod and she did as he said, opening the cover and turning to the first page.

There were sketches inside. Pencil drawings made by his hand, the first dating to the very day that she had given the journal to him. *His eighteenth birthday. Exactly four years ago.*

'I don't understand,' Mary said, her eyes wet as she looked from the page to him.

Alexander smiled and gestured back towards the journal. 'To prove it's not a lie,' he said, 'and that it's true: I have always loved you.'

She turned back to the drawings then. *Soft, but purposeful lines. Not of pity, but of joy and admiration and, above all, love.* The journal, page-by-page until its end, was filled with drawings of her.

'This one—' Alexander drew her attention to a side profile, 'whenever we all watched a film together in the sitting room. You, in the projector light.'

Mary laughed and, swiping the skin under her eyes, allowed him to direct her towards the next.

'Another—' he said, flicking through a couple of pages and stopping her again, 'the Christmas your father fell asleep on the sofa in the middle of the game.'

'He does that every year,' she replied, laughing, crying still. Careful not to dampen the paper, she pressed her finger to Alexander's drawing. It was her own hand, holding a playing card.

'I want you to have it,' Alexander said, raising his eyes so as to meet hers.

Mary shook her head. 'It was your birthday present.'

'And,' he replied, smiling, 'I appreciated it very much. But, I want to give it back to you now. After all—' a laugh and he touched her chin. 'It's my birthday again, so I can do whatever I want.'

She laughed and, touching his hand, holding it against her own face, she nodded. 'Okay. Thank you.'

'You're welcome,' Alexander smiled.

At that, Mary returned to the journal, delicately turning through the pages. Sketch after sketch, some of her face, side, front, silhouette, others of small parts of her, an eye, a hand, her hair, *he had looked at me once, twice, three times, more times than can be counted.* Then, at the end of the journal, a different sort of picture. Painted in colour, a full-page portrait dominated the final page. Her hair loose, she was wearing a red dress, the very same colour as sweet wine, with delicate spaghetti straps and fluttering off-the-shoulder sleeves. Like all the others, it was dated. *New Year's. The New Year's before he left.*

'I don't ever want to be apart from you.'

Pulling her eyes from the painting, Mary looked up at him.

'Not again,' Alexander continued. 'So, you're going to have to come back with me. To university—' She went to say something but he stopped her. 'No, you have to. Otherwise I won't— I can't go back.'

Smiling, Mary shook her head. 'I wasn't going to protest, Alex.' A laugh and, closing the journal, she set it down on the blanket next to them. 'I wasn't going to protest.'

At that, both now laughing, he drew her to him, determined never to let her go.

# Also by Quintus H. Gould

***The Lie of Innocence***

The Homestead

***The Lie of Innocence Short Stories***

1: Strawberry

www.ingramcontent.com/pod-product-compliance
Lightning Source LLC
Chambersburg PA
CBHW060538310726
48982CB00009B/1299/J

* 9 7 8 1 7 3 9 2 1 7 2 4 2 *